D0699878

THE ICE VIRGIN

Hans Christian Andersen

THE ICE VIRGIN

Translated from the Danish
and with an afterword by
PAUL BINDING

THE OVERLOOK PRESS
New York, NY

This edition first published in hardcover in the United States in 2017 by
The Overlook Press, Peter Mayer Publishers, Inc.

141 Wooster Street
New York, NY 10012
www.overlookpress.com
For bulk and special sales please email sales@overlookny.com,
or write us at the above address.

The original text of this work can be found on www.adl.dk
(Arkiv for Dansk Litteratur) and on www.andersen.sdu.dk

Cataloging-in-Publication Data is available from the Library of Congress.

Manufactured in the United States of America

ISBN: 978-1-4683-1489-2

1 3 5 7 9 8 6 4 2

This translation is for
Carol and Jock Wright

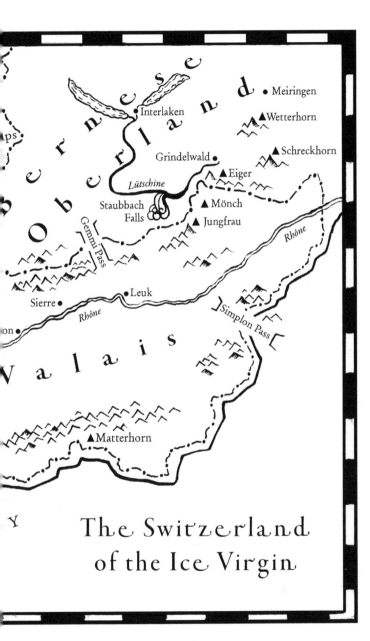

The Switzerland
of the Ice Virgin

THE ICE VIRGIN

1. Little Rudy

L ET'S VISIT SWITZERLAND, let's look round that stupendous mountain country where forests grow up sheer walls of rock. Let's climb up to dazzling snowfields, and then go down again to green meadows where rivers and streams roar along as though afraid they won't reach the sea in time and get away. The sun blazes down into the deep valley; it blazes up above too, on the hard masses of snow, with the result that over the ages they fuse into glistening blocks of ice and form rolling avalanches or piled-up glaciers. Two such glaciers lie inside the wide ravines below the Schreckhorn and the Wetterhorn, near the little mountain town of Grindelwald. So extraordinary are they to look at that many foreigners come here in summer from all countries of the world. They arrive over the high snow-covered mountains, they arrive from below, from the deep valleys, and then have to climb uphill several hours, and as they're climbing, the valley beneath sinks ever deeper; they look down into it as if viewing it from an air balloon. High up, the clouds often hang like thick, heavy curtains of smoke round the mountain peaks, while down in the valley, where the many brown chalets are scattered, a ray of sunshine is still giving light, picking out a spot in brilliant green as though it were transparent. Water roars, hums and whistles down below, water trickles and chimes up above; there it appears like fluttering silver ribbons down over the rock.

On both sides of the road up here stand cottages built of logs. Every cottage has its little potato-garden, and this is a necessity, because behind the doors are many mouths; it's full to bursting here with children, and they have insatiable appetites for food. They swarm forward from all the cottages, thrusting themselves in front of travellers whether these come on foot or by coach. The entire pack of children is intent on business. The little ones offer beautifully carved wooden chalets for sale, just like those you see built here in the mountains. Whether it's rainy weather or sunshine, the swarm of children comes forth with its wares.

Some twenty years ago, there'd be standing here every so often, but always somewhat apart from the other children, a little boy who also wanted to engage in business. He'd stand there with such an earnest expression and with both hands clenching his wooden box as if he didn't really want to let go of it. But it was precisely this earnestness, and the boy's being so little, that made him noticed and actually called upon, and he often made the best sales of anybody; he himself didn't know why. Higher up on the mountain lived his maternal grandfather who carved the delicate, appealing chalets, and up there in his living-room was an old cupboard chock-full of carvings of all kinds: nutcrackers, knives, forks, and boxes patterned with charming leaf tracery and leaping chamois. Everything to delight the eyes of children was there, but the little boy – Rudy was his name – looked with greater pleasure and longing at the old gun beneath the roof-beam. It would one day be his, his grandfather had said, but first he must become big and strong enough to use it.

Small as the boy was, he was put in charge of minding the goats, and if being able to scramble about alongside them is being a good goatherd, well then yes, Rudy was a good goatherd. He even climbed a bit higher than his charges; he liked getting birds' nests from high in the trees. He was adventurous and plucky, but you saw him smile only when he was standing beside the roaring waterfall or when he heard an avalanche rumble. He never played with the other children; he got together with them only when his grandfather sent him down to make sales, something Rudy didn't much care for. Rather he preferred clambering about by himself on the mountainside, or sitting in his grandfather's house and listening to him tell stories about old times and the breed of people nearby in Meiringen where he was from. Those people had not been living there from the first age of the world's history, Grandfather said, they'd arrived later as migrants. They'd come from far up in the north where their kinsfolk still lived and were called 'Swedes'. It took great wisdom to know this, and now Rudy knew it too! But he acquired even more wisdom from his other regular associates, the household's members of the animal family. There was a large dog, Ajola, an inheritance from Rudy's father, and a tomcat. He in particular was of great importance to Rudy; he'd taught him to climb.

'Come with me out onto the roof!' the cat had said, quite distinctly and comprehensibly, because when you're a child and can't talk, you can understand chickens and ducks, cats and dogs completely. They speak to us every bit as intelligibly as Father or Mother do, you simply have really to be a child for this to be so. Even Grandfather's walking-stick can emit neighs, can turn into a horse with head, legs and tail. In the cases of some children this comprehension recedes later than in others, and people say of these that they're backward, that they're staying children an unconscionably long time. People say such a lot of things!

'Come with me, little Rudy, out onto the roof!' was about the first thing the cat said and Rudy understood. 'Falling down's all imagination. You don't fall when you're not frightened of doing so. Come on, place one back paw – so! Then the other – like this! Now stretch out your front paws. Have your eyes skinned, and your limbs nimble. If a gap appears, just jump, keeping a good grip of yourself! That's what I do.'

And that's what Rudy did too. So he'd often be sitting on the ridge of the roof together with the cat, and sitting with him in the treetop, and yes, high up on the edge of the precipice as well, where the cat himself would not venture.

'Higher! Higher!' said the trees and bushes, 'Look at where *we* climb up to, how high up *we* reach, how tightly we cling to the furthest little pinnacles of rock!'

And Rudy would make his way up the mountain, often before the sun reached so far up, and there he'd take his morning-drink, that drink which only Our Lord can brew. But ordinary mortals can read the recipe for it, which is as follows: the fresh scent of the mountain's herbs and the valley's curly mint and thyme. The overhanging clouds absorb everything heavy into themselves, and then the winds pull them through the spruce forests. The essence of the scent turns into air, gentle, fresh air, getting ever fresher; this was Rudy's morning-drink.

The sunbeams, the daughters of the sun who bring blessings with them, would kiss his cheeks, and Dizziness herself would stand by in wait for him but not daring to come close.

And the swallows from his grandfather's house, who had no fewer than seven nests there, flew up to him and the goats, singing: 'We and you! You and us!' They brought him greetings from his home, even from the two hens, whom Rudy didn't have much to do with.

Even though he was so young, he had travelled, and not such a short distance either for a nipper like him. He was born over in Canton Valais, and taken across the mountains to here. Recently he'd gone on foot to visit the nearby Staubbach Falls, which billow like a silver veil in front of that snow-clad, dazzling white mountain, the Jungfrau (the Virgin). And in Grindelwald he'd come into contact with the great glacier, but that is a tragic story; it was there his mother met her death: 'It was there that little Rudy,' said his grandfather, 'got all his child's merriness knocked out of him. Why, when the boy wasn't so much as a year old, he laughed more than he cried – that's what his mother once wrote. But ever since he found himself inside the ice chasm, quite another disposition has got into him.' His grandfather didn't as a rule talk much about all this, but the entire mountainside knew the facts of the case.

Rudy's father had been, as we know, a mail-coach man. The large dog now at Rudy's home had always accompanied him on his route over the Simplon down to the Lake of Geneva. Rudy's family on his father's side still lived in the Rhône Valley, in Canton Valais; his paternal uncle was a seasoned chamois-hunter and a well-respected mountain guide. Rudy was only a year old when he lost his father, and his mother very much wanted to take her little child back home to her own family in the Bernese Oberland. Her father lived some hours' distance from Grindelwald; he carved in wood, and earned so much that he could support himself pretty comfortably. In the month of June, carrying her little child, she set off in the company of two chamois-hunters, taking the homewards route over the Gemmi Pass to reach Grindelwald. Already they'd done the longest stretch of the journey, and had reached the snowline by way of the mountain ridge's highest point. Already they were within sight of her native valley, with all its familiar scattered wooden chalets. There remained now only the hazard of going over the topmost section of the one great glacier.

Freshly fallen snow lay all around, and covered a ravine, not right to the bottom where the water was roaring along, but nonetheless to a depth greater than a man's height. The young woman with her child in her arms slipped, fell in and was gone. They heard no scream, not even a groan, but they did hear a little child crying. More than an hour went by before her two hunter-escorts managed to fetch, from the nearest house down below, ropes and poles which might possibly be of help. And after tremendous effort two dead bodies (as it seemed) were hauled up from the ice chasm. Every means was employed, and the men succeeded in bringing the child back to life, but not the mother. And so the old grandfather came to have a daughter's son instead of a daughter in his home, the little child who laughed more than he cried. But it seemed now as if he'd been broken of this habit. The change in him had almost certainly occurred inside the crevasse, in the cold eerie world of ice where the souls of the damned are locked up till Judgement Day, as the Swiss countryman believes.

Not unlike rushing water that's been frozen and then pressed into green blocks of glass, the glacier lies down there, one huge lump of ice tipped onto another. In the depths the furious flow of melted snow and ice roars along; deep caves, mighty chasms appear. An extraordinary glass palace it all is, and inside this the Ice Virgin lives, the glacier queen. She, the deadly, the destructive one, is half child of the air, half the river's powerful mistress, which is why she can outpace the chamois up on the snow-mountains' loftiest peaks, where even the most adventurous mountaineers have to hew steps in the ice for themselves as footholds. She sails down the torrential river on a slender spray of spruce, and leaps from boulder to boulder, her long snow-white hair fluttering around her and her blue-green coat gleaming like the water in the deep Swiss lakes.

'Go on – crush! Take a hard grip! Power belongs to me!' she says; 'they stole a beautiful boy from me, a boy I had kissed, but not kissed to death. He is back among humankind, minding the goats on the mountain, scrambling upwards, always upwards, away from all the other children – but not away from *me*. He is mine, and I will get him!'

And she ordered Her Dizziness to carry out errands on her behalf. In summer it was too muggy for the Ice Virgin to stay outside where the curly mint thrives. Dizziness rose up and then ducked down; but next appeared first one, then three emanations of this spirit, for Dizziness has many sisters, a whole tribe of them. And the Ice Virgin chose the strongest of all the ones who prevail indoors and out-of-doors alike. They sit on banisters and balustrades, they scamper like a squirrel along the mountain-edge, they jump out in front of you and tread air as the swimmer treads water, and entice their victim forth, and so down into the abyss. Both Dizziness and the Ice Virgin grab at human beings the way the polyp grabs at everything that moves within its reach.

'*Me* grab *him*!' said Dizziness, 'No, I'm not able to do *that*! The cat, that wretch, has taught him his own tricks. The human child has enough power of his own to keep me away. Why, I can't even get near the little lad when he hangs on a branch over the precipice and I'm right there taking the trouble to tickle the soles of his feet or giving him a ducking in the air. I simply can't do it!'

'We *can* do it!' said the Ice Virgin, 'you and me! Me! Me!'

'No, no!' This last rang out as if it were the mountain echo of church bells ringing, but it was the song, the speech, the chorus of all the other spirits of nature blending together, gentle, loving and good: the daughters of the sunbeams. Every evening they lie down in a circle on the mountain peaks, spreading out their rose-coloured wings which, as the sun sinks, flush ever more deeply red. The high Alps are aglow, people actually call it 'the alpenglow'. When the sun has set, the daughters go onto the tops of the mountains, into the white snow, and sleep there till the sun rises, when they can emerge once again. They're particularly fond of flowers, butterflies and human beings, and among all these they've specially singled out Rudy. 'You won't capture him! You'll never have him!' they said.

'I've captured and kept far bigger and stronger human beings!' said the Ice Virgin.

Then the sun's daughters sang a song about the wanderer whose cloak the whirlwind seized and carried off in its furious flight. The wind took the outer covering away but not the man himself. 'You, Force's children, can grab Rudy all you want, but you'll never be able to hold onto him. He is stronger, he is more soulful, even than ourselves. He climbs higher than the sun, our mother. He is in possession of the magic word which is binding on wind and water so that they have to serve and obey him. You just loosen all the heaviness and oppression of his weight and he'll rise up higher still.'

That's how the chorus rang out, beautifully, like a peal of bells!

And every morning the sunbeams shone in through the one little window in the grandfather's house, in on the peaceful child. The sunbeams' daughters kissed him, they wanted to thaw out, to warm away, to expel those kisses of ice the glacier's Royal Virgin had given him when he lay in his dead mother's lap in the deep ice chasm and was rescued from it as by a miracle.

2. Journey to the new home

And now Rudy was eight years old. His uncle in the Rhône Valley, on the far side of the mountains, wanted to take the boy into his own home. He could be educated better there, and get a good start in life. His grandfather realised this, and so let him go.

Rudy was about to leave. There were several, other than his grandfather, he had to say goodbye to. First there was Ajola, the old dog.

'Your father was a mail-coach man, and I was a mail-coach dog!' Ajola said, 'we travelled up and down the country, so I know the dogs and the people over on the other side of the mountains. It's never been my custom to talk a lot, but now when we haven't long to talk to each other, I'll talk more than I usually do. I'll tell you a story that I've long gone and chewed over. I can't understand it, and possibly you won't either. But that doesn't matter, because I've got something out of it – that things aren't so fairly distributed in this world either for dogs or for humans. Not all dogs are made to sit on knees or lap up milk. It wasn't my lot to do such things. But I have seen a puppy ride in a carriage, in a seat meant for a human being. The woman who was his owner – or who was owned by *him* – carried with her a flask full of milk which she gave him to drink from. She'd also got some sugared bread for him, but he never bothered about eating it, just sniffed at it, and so she ate it up herself. But me, I was running through the mire by the side of the wagon as hungry as any dog can get. I've chewed all this over in my thoughts, that it wasn't as it should be, but such a lot isn't – everywhere. I hope, Rudy, you'll be able to sit on someone's knee or ride in a carriage, but you can't make that happen by yourself; I haven't managed it, either by barking or by yowling.'

That was Ajola's speech, and Rudy hugged his neck and kissed him on his wet nose, and then he took the cat in his arms, but the cat wriggled free. 'You've become too strong for me, and I certainly don't want to use my claws on you. Just you go and climb over the mountains. I have taught you how to climb. Never believe you're going to fall, and keep a good grip on yourself.' And then the cat ran off, because he didn't want to let Rudy see the grief shining in his eyes.

The two hens were running round on the floor; one of them had lost her tail. A tourist who fancied himself a hunter had shot her tail off because he'd taken the hen for some bird of prey.

'Rudy's going over the mountains!' said one hen.

'He's always in a hurry!' said the other, 'and I don't like saying goodbye.' And the two of them scuttled off.

He also said goodbye to the goats, and they called out: 'May you... may we... may... maaa!' and it was all so sad.

Two experienced guides from the local community were about to cross the mountains. They would be going down the other side by the Gemmi Pass. So Rudy went with them – and on foot. It was a tough trek for so little a lad, but Rudy had strength and courage which didn't ever wane.

The swallows flew part of the way with them. 'We and you! You and us!' they sang. The guides' route took them over the fast-flowing Lütschine River which tumbles out in many little streams from the black ravine of the Grindelwald glacier. Loose tree-trunks and bits of rock served as bridge here. Now they were over by the alder thicket and beginning to go up the mountain close to where the glacier had worked loose from the mountainside. And next they went actually out onto the glacier, over blocks of ice, and out round them too. Rudy had to crawl for a little, then walk for a little. His eyes shone with pure pleasure, and in this spirit he stepped with his iron-clasped mountain-boots so firmly as though to put down markers for his movements. The black churned-up earth which the mountain stream had emptied over the glacier gave it a calcified appearance, but blue-green, glassy ice shone through nonetheless. They had to go round small pools rimmed by pressed ice-blocks, and in doing so approached a huge boulder that was swaying on the brink of a fissure in the ice. The boulder toppled over, fell, rolled down and released the echo that rang from the glacier's deep hollow passageways.

On up! Always they went upwards. The glacier stretched above them like a river of wildly piled-up ice masses squeezed between precipitous rocks. For a split second Rudy thought about what he'd been told, how he had lain with his mother inside one of these cold-exhaling ravines, but such thoughts quickly went away. For him it was just another story out of all the many he had heard. Every now and again, when the men thought climbing was a bit too difficult for the little chap, they extended their hands to him, but he did not become too exhausted, and on the smooth ice he stood as steadily as a chamois. Presently they came out onto rocky ground, now between moss-free stones, now in amongst low spruce trees, and then out again into green pasture, ever changing, ever new. All round rose the great snow-covered mountains, Jungfrau (the Virgin), Mönch (the Monk) and Eiger (the Ogre). Rudy had never been as high as this before, never trodden the sea of snow now opening up before him. It lay with motionless waves of snow which the wind had blown into shape out of single flakes, just as it blows the foam from the waters of the sea. Glacier after glacier hold each other by the hand, if one might say that. Each one is a glass palace for the Ice Virgin whose power and intention it is to capture and entomb.

The sun blazed intensely down. The snow was truly dazzling and as though studded with blue-white, sparkling splinters of diamond. Innumerable insects, particularly butterflies and bees, lay dead in heaps on the snow. They had ventured too high up, or else the wind had borne them to the point where they expired in this cold. About the Wetterhorn a threatening cloud hung like a fine-woven black tuft of wool. It descended, swelling with what lurked within, a Föhn, violent in its strength were it to break loose. The impression of the whole journey, the night-camp up here, and the path going onwards, the deep mountain chasms where the water for a staggeringly long period of time had sawn through the blocks of stone, fixed itself indelibly on Rudy's memory.

A derelict stone building on the far side of the sea of snow provided overnight shelter. Here they found charcoal and branches of spruce, the fire they lit got going quickly, and they made up bedding for the night as comfortably as possible. The men seated themselves round the fire, smoking their tobacco and drinking the warm spicy drink they had prepared for themselves. Rudy was given his share, and then talk got underway about the mysterious creatures of the alpine country: about the strange colossal snakes in the deep lakes, about the folk who come out at night, the ghostly army which carries sleeping people through the air to the marvellous floating city of Venice, about the wild shepherd who drove his black sheep across the pasture; nobody had seen these animals, but they had heard the sound of their bells and the herd's eerie baaing. Rudy listened with curiosity but without fear, something he simply did not know, and as he listened, he thought he caught the spectral hollow baaing. Yes, it became more and more distinct, the men heard it as well, stopped in the midst of their conversation, hearkened, and told Rudy that he must *not* fall asleep.

It was a Föhn blowing up, the violent storm-wind which hurls itself from the mountains down into the valley and in its viciousness breaks trees as if they were reeds, and shifts chalets from one bank of the river to the other just as we move a chess piece.

An hour had gone by before they said to Rudy that it had passed over. He could go to sleep now, and exhausted by the trek, he slept as if on command.

Early in the morning they set off again. That day the sun illuminated for Rudy new mountains, new glaciers and snowfields. They were entering Canton Valais, and were on the far side of the mountain ridge you saw from Grindelwald, though still a long way from the new home. Other mountain ravines, other pastures, woods and pathways presented themselves, other houses, other people were on view. But what people were these he was seeing? They were freaks of nature: weird, fat, jaundiced faces, the neck a heavy, hideous chunk of flesh with pouches hanging out. They were *creitins*,* they dragged themselves wretchedly about, and looked with blank eyes at any outsiders who arrived. The women looked the most frightful of all. Were these the people of his new home?

3. Rudy's uncle

In his uncle's house, where Rudy eventually arrived, the people looked, thank God, as Rudy was accustomed to seeing them. Only one solitary *creitin* was here, a poor, witless lad, one of those pitiable creatures who in their poverty and loneliness are always taken in by families in Canton Valais, staying a couple of months in every household. Poor Saperli was in just this position when Rudy arrived.

---

* Swiss-French word for those with thyroid hormone deficiency, once prevalent in southern Switzerland; hence English 'cretin' in medical usage from the late eighteenth century on.

Rudy's uncle was still an energetic huntsman and an accomplished cooper, and his wife was a small, lively person, with something of a bird's face, eagle eyes and a long, rather downy neck. Everything was new for Rudy, clothes, customs and practicalities, even the language, but this his child's ear soon learned to understand. It all looked so well-to-do here compared with his home at his grandfather's. The house his uncle and aunt lived in was larger, walls decorated with chamois horns and brightly polished guns. Over the front door hung the Madonna; fresh alpine roses and a burning lamp were placed before her.

Rudy's uncle was, as has been said, one of the region's most knowledgeable chamois-hunters, and also the best and most experienced mountain guide. Rudy would become the darling of this household, though in truth there was one of these already. This was an aged, blind and deaf hunting-dog who couldn't make himself useful any longer but had formerly done so incomparably. People remembered the animal's great abilities of earlier years, and so now he was part of the family, living with it in comfort. Rudy embraced the dog, but the dog no longer had anything to do with strangers, and this was what Rudy still was, though not for long: he soon took root in the household and in people's hearts.

'Things are not so bad here in Canton Valais!' said his uncle, 'we have chamois; they haven't died out so soon as the ibex. It's far better here now than in the old time. However much they say in praise of that, our own is much better. The bag's had a hole punched in it, and fresh air has got into our shut-off valley. Something better always emerges when the old and decrepit fall,' he said, and Uncle became really talkative when he spoke about his childhood years, which were his own father's heyday, when Valais was, as he put it, a closed bag containing far too many sick people, pathetic *creitins*. 'But then the French soldiers came along, they were real doctors, they were; straight-away they put down sickness pretty thoroughly, and sick persons too. The Frenchmen know how to give blows all right, they can deal knock-out blows of many different kinds, and their girls know how to knock you out too.' And so saying his uncle nodded to his French-born wife and laughed. 'The French even dealt blows to the stones so that they surrendered. They struck the Simplon Pass out of the rocks and knocked a roadway into shape right up there, so that now I can say to a three-year-old child: 'Take a walk down into Italy, just keep to the main road!' – and the young 'un will find his way down into Italy sure enough, just by sticking to the highway.' And accordingly Rudy's uncle sang a French song and shouted out: 'Hurrah for Napoleon Bonaparte.'

Then it was that Rudy first heard about France, about Lyons, the great city on the River Rhône, which his uncle had been to.

It wouldn't be many years before Rudy became a clever chamois-hunter himself, he had a real flare, said his uncle, and he taught him how to handle a gun, how to take aim and shoot. In the hunting season he took him into the mountains, getting him to drink warm chamois blood because it keeps dizziness at bay from the hunter. He taught him how to tell the time when, on the various mountainsides, the avalanches would roll, at midday or in the evening, according to how the sun cast its beams. He taught him to pay careful attention to the chamois themselves, and learn from the way they leaped, so that you fell on your feet and stood firm. And if in a mountain ravine there wasn't support for your feet, then you had to look for supports for your elbows, and cling on tight with every muscle you had in your thigh or calf. Even the nape of the neck could hold on firmly if it were necessary. The chamois were clever, they'd position their own kind as forerunners. But the hunter has to be cleverer still and put the animals off the scent. He can deceive them too, he can hang his coat and hat on an alpenstock, and the chamois will take the clothes for the man himself. This trick his uncle played one day when he was on a hunt with Rudy.

The mountain-path was narrow, there really wasn't one at all; a thin ledge, it was close to the dizzying precipice. The snow was half thawed out, the stone crumbled when you trod on it, his uncle therefore lay with the whole length of his body on the ground and crawled forwards. Every stone that broke off dropped, knocking against others, then bounced and rolled again, causing many others also to bounce from rock-wall to rock-wall, before coming to a stop in the black depth below. Rudy was standing a hundred paces from his uncle, on the furthest firm pinnacle of rock, and saw coming through the air, to hover over his uncle, a powerful vulture, which with one blow from its wings would hurl the crawling worm into the precipice to turn him into carrion.

Uncle had eyes only for the chamois which, with her young kid, was in view on the far side of the chasm. Rudy fastened his gaze on the bird, realised what it meant to do, and therefore put his hand on his gun to shoot. When the chamois sped off, Uncle fired, and the parent animal was killed with one deadly bullet, but her kid, the poor young animal, ran away, as though to show and to overcome the fact that its whole life consisted of flight from danger. The gigantic bird, terrified by the bang, opted for another route. Rudy's uncle did not know the danger he'd been in; he heard of it first from Rudy.

As now, in the best of spirits, they made their way home, his uncle whistling a song from his boyhood, a strange noise suddenly boomed out not far away. They looked to the side of them, they looked upwards, and there, way up on the sloping mountain ledge, the snow coverlet was heaving; it was billowing just like a stretched piece of linen when the wind gets in under it. The rippling heights above them were being smashed up as if they were marble slabs, which then burst and let loose frothing, tumbling waters, resounding all round like a muffled thunderclap. It was an avalanche which was falling, not down over Rudy and his uncle, but near them, far too near them.

'Hold tight, Rudy!' Uncle shouted, 'as tight as you can manage!'

And Rudy grasped the tree-trunk close to him. His uncle scrambled over him up into the branches of the tree and clung on fast, while the avalanche moved down many yards away from them. But its aftershock, the gusts of storm-wind in its train, broke up and extensively laid into all the trees and bushes as if they were dry reeds, and flung them far and wide. Rudy lay face pressed down on the ground. The tree-trunk he'd taken hold of was as if it had been sawn through and its crown hurled a good distance away. There among the broken branches lay his uncle with his head crushed. His hands were still warm, his face was quite unrecognisable. Rudy stood by him pale and trembling. This was his first experience of fear, the first moment of horror he'd faced.

He came back in the late evening with tidings of death to a home which was now a house of mourning. Its mistress stood there without a word, without a tear, and not till the dead body was brought in did she give vent to her anguish. The poor *creitin* crept up to his bed; he wasn't seen for the whole of that day. Then towards evening he came to Rudy:

'Write a letter for me! Saperli doesn't know how to write! Saperli can go with the letter to the post-office.'

'A letter from you?' asked Rudy, 'who to?'

'To the Lord Christ!'

'Who do you mean by that?'

And the half-wit, as they called the *creitin*, gave Rudy a pleading look, clasped his hands, and said so solemnly and piously: 'Jesus Christ. Saperli will send him a letter, praying to him that Saperli should lie dead and not the man of this house.'

And Rudy shook him by the hand. 'That letter wouldn't ever reach him! That letter wouldn't ever give us him back.'

Rudy found it hard to explain the impossibility to him.

'Now you are the mainstay of the house!' said Rudy's foster-mother, and that's what he became.

4. Babette

'Who is the best shot in Canton Valais?' Yes, the chamois knew! 'Watch out for Rudy!' they'd say. 'Who's the best-looking shot?' 'Rudy, of course!' the girls said, but they didn't say: 'Watch out for Rudy.' Dutiful mothers didn't say it either, because he nodded to them in as friendly a way as he did to the young girls. He was so cheerful and happy; his cheeks had a tan, his teeth were a healthy white, and his eyes shone coal-black. He was a handsome young man, and only twenty years old. Icy water didn't bite him with its cold when he was swimming; he could turn himself about in the water like a fish. He could cling to rock-walls like a snail; he had first-class muscles and sinews, and showed this when jumping; the cat had been his first teacher, and the chamois next. The best mountain guide to entrust with your life was Rudy, he could have amassed an entire fortune this way. The cooper's craft, something else his uncle had taught him, he had no interest in: his pleasure and his yearning centred on shooting chamois; this also brought in money. Rudy was a good match, they said, if only he wouldn't set his sights above his own station. At the dance he was a dancer all the girls dreamed about; and through their waking hours, one after the other, they went about thinking of him.

'He kissed me at the dance!' said the schoolteacher's Annette to her dearest friend, but she shouldn't have said this – even to her dearest friend. Such a thing isn't easy to keep to yourself; it's like sand in a bag full of holes; it leaks out. Soon, no matter how good-natured and honourable Rudy was, everyone knew he kissed at the dance. And yet he hadn't kissed at all the one he most wanted to have kissed.

'Watch him!' said an old huntsman, 'he's kissed Annette, he's begun with 'A', and now he'll kiss his way down the whole alphabet.'

One kiss at one dance was all as yet that gossip could relay about Rudy, but kissed Annette he had, and she was not in the least the flower of his heart.

Down in Bex, between large walnut trees, close by a fast-flowing little mountain stream, lived the rich miller. His home was a big edifice of three storeys, with small turrets roofed with wooden shingles and studded with plates of sheet-metal which shone in both sun- and moonlight. The largest turret had for weather-vane a gleaming arrow piercing an apple, which was meant to represent Wilhelm Tell's feat of archery. The mill had a prosperous, well-kept appearance, and lent itself to being sketched or written about, but the miller's daughter defied being drawn or described, at least that's what Rudy would say, and yet she stood pictured in his heart, from inside which her eyes were sending out enough beams to start a whole fire. It had all come about quite suddenly, just as the other kind of fire can make its appearance, and the extraordinary thing about it was that the miller's daughter, the lovely Babette, had no idea of all this, she and Rudy having exchanged not so much as a couple of words.

The miller was wealthy, and this wealth meant that Babette was placed very high to get at socially. But nothing is situated so high, said Rudy to himself, that you can't reach it; you've got to climb, and you don't fall down if you don't think you will. This wisdom he had from his earliest home.

Now it happened that Rudy had business to do in Bex, which was a good journey away. At that time the railway had still not been brought to these parts. From the Rhône glacier beneath the foot of the Simplon, flanked by many, ever changing high mountains, the Rhône Valley stretches with its mighty river, the Rhône, which often becomes swollen, flooding field and road, ruining everything. Between the towns of Sion and St Maurice the valley curves round, bending like an elbow, and below St Maurice is so contracted it has room only for the river-bed and the narrow carriageway.

An old tower, like a frontier-post of Canton Valais, which ends here, stands on the mountainside, looking out across the brick-walled bridge to the toll-gate on the opposite bank where Canton Vaud begins – and the nearest town, not far distant, is Bex. Once on this side, with every step you take forwards, affluence and fecundity are more apparent; you are in a veritable garden of chestnuts and walnut trees; here and there cypresses peep out and pomegranate flowers burst forth. The warmth of the South is here, it's as if you've arrived in Italy.

Rudy got to Bex, attended to his business, took a look round, but he didn't see any mill-hand, let alone Babette herself. Things were not as they should be.

Evening came on, the air was full of the fragrance of wild thyme and blossoming lime trees. A sort of shimmery, light blue veil lay over the forest-green mountains, there was an all-pervasive stillness which did not relate to sleep or death. No, it was as if the whole natural world were holding its breath, as though placing itself in position for a photograph to be taken against the background of blue sky. Here and there among the trees, above the green fields, poles stood supporting telegraph wires which had been stretched through the quiet valley. Against one of these an object was leaning so motionless that you could well believe it to be a dead tree-trunk. But it was Rudy who was standing as completely still as his surroundings of this moment. He was not asleep, even less was he dead, but just as great world events and those moments in life of real consequence to the individual very often go flying through the telegraph wires without the wire indicating this with a quiver or a sound, so there went passing through Rudy now powerful, overwhelming thoughts, how to be happy in life his constant preoccupation from now on.

His eyes were focused on a point amongst the foliage, a light in the miller's living quarters where Babette lived. So still did Rudy stand you could well believe he was aiming to shoot a chamois, but at that moment he himself was like a chamois, which in a matter of moments can be standing as though hewn out of the mountain, and then suddenly, at the rolling of a stone, takes a huge leap and gallops away. And that's just what happened to Rudy; a thought went rolling through him.

'Never say die!' he said, 'Go to the mill! Say "Good evening!" to the miller and "Good day to you!" to Babette. You don't fall when you don't think you're going to. Babette has only to see me this once for me to be her man!'

And Rudy laughed, felt good in himself, and went round to the mill. He knew what he wanted; he wanted to have Babette.

The river with its yellowy-white water sped past, the willow trees and limes hung over the scurrying water. Rudy approached by the pathway, and as it says in the old children's song:

'In the miller's house there was no one to see
Except a little pussycat looking at me!'

The household cat stood on the front steps, arched his back, and said: 'Miaow!' But Rudy was in no mood for talk. He knocked on the door; nobody heard, nobody opened up. 'Miaow!' said the cat. Had Rudy been a child once again, he'd have understood what the animal was saying, and would have heard the cat telling him: 'There's nobody at home!' He had now to go over to the mill and make enquiries there; he then left a message. The master had gone travelling, a long way away, to the town of Interlaken, 'inter lacus, between the lakes' as the schoolteacher, Annette's father, had explained out of his great store of learning. The miller and with him

Babette were far away; there was a great shooting contest, which would start the very next day and last eight whole days. Swiss from all the German-speaking cantons would be coming to it.

Poor Rudy, you could say this was not his luckiest day. He'd come over to Bex, and what could he do now but make his way home again? And this is what he did, taking the road through St Maurice and Sion back into his own valley, his own mountains. But he was not down-hearted. When the sun rose the next morning his spirits were high to match; in truth they'd never been low.

'Babette's in Interlaken, many days' journey from here,' he said to himself, 'it's a long way over there if you keep to the beaten track, to the highway. But it's not so long if you haul yourself across the mountains, and isn't that just the route for a chamois-hunter? It's a route I've travelled before, anyway. Over there's my childhood home, where I lived when I was little with Grandfather. And they're having a shooting contest in Interlaken. I'll take first prize at it, and I'll be in the very same place too as Babette – once I've made her acquaintance.'

With his light knapsack, in which he'd packed his Sunday best, with his rifle and his hunter's bag, Rudy went up onto the mountain, going the short way which was nevertheless really rather long. But the shooting contest had begun only that day, and would last the whole week. He'd heard that the miller and Babette would be staying with their relations in Interlaken. Up over the Gemmi Pass Rudy went; he would descend to Grindelwald.

Feeling on top of the world, he strode along, up into the fresh, light, invigorating mountain air. The valley sank beneath ever lower, the horizon ahead became ever wider. A snowy peak rose here, a snowy peak rose there, and soon appeared the shining white row of the high Alps. Rudy knew every snow-capped mountain. He steered his course by the Schreckhorn which lifted its white-powdered stone finger high into the blue air.

At last he was over the high ridge; the pastures were now sloping down towards the valley of his old home; the air was light, his mind felt light. Mountain and valley were full of flowers and greenery, his heart was full of youth's ideals: you will never get old, you will never die – live, do what you want, enjoy yourself! – free as a bird, light as a bird, that's how Rudy was. And the swallows flew past and sang as they'd done in his childhood: 'We and you, and you and us!' Everything was release and joy.

Down below, the velvet green meadow lay bestrewn with brown timber chalets; the River Lütschine hummed and roared. He saw the glacier with its glass-green edges in the grubby snow, he saw the deep crevasses, the topmost and bottommost glacier. The bells rang out across to him from the church, as if they wanted to welcome him home. His heart beat more strongly and enlarged to measure, so that Babette disappeared from it for a moment, so greatly had his heart expanded, so full of memories.

He was back again on that road where, as a little lad, he used to stand with the other children on its ditch-like kerb, selling carvings of chalets. Up there, behind the spruce trees, his grandfather's house still stood; strangers lived there. Children came running onto the road; they wanted to engage in business; one of them held out an Alpine rose; Rudy took it as a favourable omen, and thought afresh of Babette.

Soon he was down over the bridge where the two Lütschine rivers converge; the deciduous trees were increasing now, the walnut trees provided shade. Now he saw flags waving, the white cross on red bunting that both the Swiss and the Danish have – and before him lay Interlaken.

It was a truly magnificent town, like no other, so thought Rudy. A Swiss town in holiday attire, it was different from the other provincial towns, which were a whole lot of heavy stone houses, oppressive, alien, condescending. No, here looked as though the chalets from up in the mountains had simply been transported down to the green valley beside the clear, rapid river, and had then fallen into line, if a little unevenly, to form a street. And the most magnificent of all streets had certainly sprung up since Rudy, who'd then been a small boy, was here last. It might have been brought into existence by all the delightful chalets which Grandfather had carved, and of which the cupboard at home had been full, being lined up here and then growing sturdier, like the most ancient of old chestnut trees. Every house was a hotel, to use the new term, with carved woodwork on the windows and balconies, jutting-out roofs, very neat and trim, and in front of every house a whole flower-garden, stretching to the broad, macadamed roadway. The houses ranged the whole length of the street, but on one side of it only; otherwise they'd have hidden the fresh green meadow directly in front, where the cattle had bells which clanged as though they were up in the high alpine pastures. The meadow was framed by high mountains which had seemingly parted in the middle so that from here you could see the shining, snow-clad Jungfrau properly, the most beautifully shaped of all the Swiss mountains.

What a throng of elegant ladies and gentlemen from foreign countries, what a swarm of country folk from the different cantons! The marksmen carried the number of their place in the contest in a garland round their hats. There was music and song, there were barrel-organs and wind instruments, shouting and clamour. Houses and bridges were decorated with verses and emblems; flags and banners waved, the bangs from shot after shot rang out. That was the best music to Rudy's ears, and in all this he completely forgot Babette, for whose sake he had come here.

The marksmen shoved their way to the target-shooting. Rudy was soon among them, and the most skilful and the happiest; he always hit the black spots at the targets' centres.

'Whoever is that stranger, that very young huntsman?' people asked. 'He speaks French just as they do in Canton Valais. But he also gives a good account of himself in our German,' said some others, 'As a child he lived here in these parts, near Grindelwald,' one of them knew.

There was certainly life in the fellow. His eyes shone, his sight and aim were sure, therefore he scored. Good fortune gives us courage, and courage Rudy had always had in plenty. Soon he'd already made a circle of friends for himself here, he became both honoured and acclaimed. Babette was as good as clean gone from his thoughts. Then a heavy hand clapped him on the shoulder, and a bluff voice addressed him in French:

'Are you from Canton Valais?'

Rudy turned round and saw a red, hearty-expressioned face, a bulky fellow: the miller from Bex. With his broad body he all but blocked the delicate, dainty Babette from view, who even so peeked out at Rudy with gleaming dark eyes. The rich miller was tickled pink it was a hunter from a French canton who had made the best shots, and was the one receiving the honours. Rudy was truly a child of fortune. What he had travelled all this way to find, but had come near to forgetting, was actually seeking him out.

When you're a long way from home and meet up with people from your own part of the world, you get acquainted on the spot, and start chatting to one another. Rudy was top man at this shooting festival thanks to his shots, likewise the miller back in Bex was top man thanks to his money and his flourishing mill. And so the two men shook hands as they'd never done before; Babette also took Rudy by the hand so unaffectedly that he took hers again, and looked at her, making her blush the deepest red.

The miller gave an account of the long route their way here had comprised, the many large towns they'd seen; the journey had been carefully planned, they'd travelled by steamer, railway and coach.

'I took the shorter route,' said Rudy, 'I went over the mountains. There's no route so high you can't take it.'

'And break your neck into the bargain!' said the miller, 'and that's something you should be mindful of: breaking your neck at some point, bold chap that you are.'

''You don't fall if you don't think you're going to!' said Rudy.

And the miller's kinsfolk in Interlaken, in whose house the miller and Babette were staying, invited Rudy to drop round and see them for a while; he was from the same canton as members of their family. Rudy appreciated this offer, good fortune was still with him, as it always is with somebody who trusts in himself, and remembers that 'Our Lord gives us nuts, but he doesn't crack them open for us!'

And Rudy sat, like one of the family, in the house of the miller's kinsfolk, and he was toasted for being the best shot, and Babette clinked glasses with him, and Rudy thanked her for doing this.

Towards evening they all walked under the walnut trees along the beautiful road with the elegant hotels, and here was such a mixed throng of people, such a great crowd that Rudy felt he should offer Babette his arm. He told her how happy he was to have come across people from Vaud, Vaud and Valais were good canton-neighbours. He expressed his happiness so sincerely that Babette felt she should give his hand a gentle squeeze. They were now virtually like old friends, and so she set out to be entertaining, this lovely little human being. It suited her so enchantingly, thought Rudy, to be pointing out what was ridiculous and extravagant about the clothes the foreign women wore and the way they behaved here, and she wasn't at all mocking them, because they were all really good people, she knew that, very nice, very likeable. She herself had a godmother who was just such a distinguished lady, an Englishwoman. Eighteen years earlier, when Babette got christened, she'd come to Bex. She had given Babette the precious brooch she wore on her breast. Twice her godmother had written to her, and this year they were to have met her with her daughters here in Interlaken; they were old ladies, Babette said, almost in their thirties. She herself was only eighteen!

The small sweet mouth didn't stop moving for a second, and everything that Babette said rang in Rudy's ears as though it were of the greatest importance. He spoke to her again, and this time what he felt he had to say he actually said: how many times he'd been to Bex, how well he knew the mill, how often he'd seen Babette, though most likely she'd never noticed him; and how, the last time he arrived at the mill, with so many thoughts he could not express, she and his father had turned out to be away, a long way away, though not so far that he couldn't haul himself over that mountain-wall that made the route so long,

Yes, he said all this, and he said much else; he told her how greatly she attracted him, and that it was for her sake, and not for the shooting contest, that he'd come here.

Babette became utterly quiet; it was almost too much to bear, what he had confided to her.

And while they were walking, the sun sank behind the high wall of mountains. The Jungfrau stood in all its splendour and glory, surrounded by the forest-green wreath of the mountains close by. Many people stopped in their tracks to look up at it; Rudy and Babette looked up at it too, in all its majesty.

'Nowhere is more beautiful than here!' said Babette.

'Nowhere!' said Rudy, and he looked at Babette.

'Tomorrow I have to go away!' he said after a short pause.

'Visit us in Bex!' whispered Babette, 'that will make my father very pleased.'

5. On the way home

Oh, what a lot Rudy had to carry the next day when he made his way home over the high mountains. Yes, he had three silver cups, two high-quality rifles, and a silver coffee-pot which would prove useful when he was setting up home.

Yet this was not what was pressing on him the most; he was carrying over the high mountains – or was *it* carrying *him*? – something weightier, still more powerful. But the weather was raw, grey, charged with rain, and oppressive; the clouds descended over the mountain heights like black mourning-crape, enveloping the gleaming summits. From the forest the last axe-blow of the day rang out, and down the side of the mountain tree-trunks rolled, looking from high up like flimsy firewood, but from nearer to like trees that had become masts for ships. The Lütschine pealed its monotonous music, the wind whistled, the clouds voyaged past. Close to Rudy a young girl appeared quite suddenly. He hadn't noticed her till she was right there beside him. She wanted to cross the mountain too. Her eyes had a peculiar power; you could look into them, they were so weirdly limpid, so deep, fathomless.

'Have you got a sweetheart?' Rudy asked. All his thoughts were filled with having a sweetheart.

'I have no one,' she said, and laughed, but it was as if what she'd said wasn't the truth. 'Let's not go a long way round. We should veer more to the left. It's shorter.'

'Yes, till you fall into an ice crevasse!' said Rudy. 'Don't you know a better way – and you wanting to be a mountain guide?'

'I know the way exactly!' she said, 'and my mind's in good trim too. Yours is still down in the valley. Up here you've got to start paying attention to the Ice Virgin – she doesn't mean human beings any good; that's what the humans themselves say!'

'I'm not afraid of *her*!' said Rudy, 'she had to let go of me when I was a child; I shall give her the slip easily enough now I'm an adult.'

And the darkness intensified, the rain was falling; snow came, it shone, it dazzled.

'Just reach your hand out to me; that way I can help you to go on up,' said the girl, and she touched him with an ice-cold finger.

'*You* help *me*!' said Rudy, 'I'm in no need of any *woman's* help when it comes to climbing, that's for sure!' And he increased his pace to get away from her. The snowstorm was coming down like a curtain all round him, the wind whistled, and then at his back he heard the girl laughing and singing, and it rang out so eerily. Presumably this was some species of troll in the Ice Virgin's service. Rudy had heard about such things when he was little and made that overnight stop up here during the crossing of the mountains.

The snowfall lessened, the cloud now lay below him. He looked behind him, there was nobody to be seen any more, but he heard laughter and yodelling, which didn't sound as though it came from a human being.

When Rudy finally reached the topmost part of the mountain, where the path began to descend to the Rhône Valley, he saw, in the clear blue strip of sky in the direction of Chamonix, two bright stars which shone so glitteringly, and he thought of Babette, of himself and his good fortune, and his thoughts warmed him.

6. The visit to the mill

'What treasures you're bringing home!' said Rudy's old foster-mother, and her strange eagle eyes flashed, and she moved her scraggy neck more quickly than ever in peculiar twists and turns. 'You've got good fortune on your side, Rudy. I must kiss you, my sweet boy!'

And Rudy let himself be kissed, but it was clear from his face that he was submitting to circumstances, domestic life's little trials! 'How good-looking you are!' said the old woman.

'Don't get me believing *that*!' said Rudy, laughing, but pleased nonetheless.

'I'll say it again,' said the old woman, 'you've got good fortune on your side!'

'Well, I agree with you there!' he said, and thought of Babette.

Never before had he longed as much as now for the deep valley.

'They must have arrived home!' he said to himself, 'it's already two days later than when they intended to be back. I must go to Bex.'

And Rudy went to Bex, and the miller and his daughter were at home. They made him very welcome, and he was given warm regards from the family in Interlaken. Babette didn't talk much, she had become quite tongue-tied, but her eyes spoke, and that was perfectly sufficient for Rudy. The miller, who normally liked to do the talking – he was accustomed to people laughing at all his quips and puns; he was the rich miller, was he not? – seemed to prefer to listen instead to Rudy recounting hunting stories: the difficulties and dangers the chamois-hunters confront up on the high mountain peaks, and how you must go down on all fours when approaching the treacherous snow cornices which wind and weather fasten to the mountain edge, and then go on all fours again when crossing those makeshift bridges the snowdrift has thrown across the deep chasms. Rudy looked so dashing as with brightly shining eyes he talked about his hunter's life, the chamois' cleverness and audacious leaps, the mighty Föhn and the rolling avalanches. He correctly noticed that with every fresh description he was winning over the miller more and more, and that what particularly appealed to him was the account of the vulture and the bold king-eagle.

Not far away, but inside Canton Valais, there was an eagle's nest built in very deftly under the overhanging edge of the mountain. There was a young bird up there, which nobody had caught. A few days earlier an Englishman had offered Rudy a whole heap of gold for capturing the young one alive. 'But there are limits to everything,' Rudy said, 'the eaglet there is simply not for taking. It would be crazy to let oneself in for such a thing.'

And the wine flowed and the conversation flowed, but the evening was all too short for Rudy, and indeed it was gone midnight when he brought this first visit to the mill to an end.

The lights shone on for a little while through the window and among the green branches. From the open hatch the Parlour Cat came out onto the roof and by way of the guttering the Kitchen Cat did the same.

'Do you know the latest news from inside the mill?' said the Parlour Cat. 'A private engagement is underway in this very house! The Old Man doesn't know about it yet. All evening long Rudy and Babette have been making contact under the table with their paws – I mean, their feet! They trod on me twice, but I didn't so much as miaow; it'd only have drawn attention.'

'*I* would have miaowed!' said the Kitchen Cat.

'Yes, but how you behave in the kitchen isn't how you behave in the parlour!' said the Parlour Cat, 'I only wonder what the miller will say when he hears about the engagement.'

Yes, what would the miller say, that was what Rudy was wondering too, but he found himself unable to wait long before knowing. And so, not many days later, when the omnibus rumbled over the Rhône bridge between Valais and Vaud, Rudy was sitting on it in as good spirits as ever, and full of pleasant thoughts about getting consent this very evening.

And when the evening had been and gone, and the omnibus was making the same way back, yes, once again Rudy was sitting on it, just as before except that at the mill the Parlour Cat was spreading news:

'Have you heard, you kitchen creature you? The miller now knows everything. It's come to a fine old pass. Rudy arrived here towards evening, and he and Babette had a great deal to huddle together and whisper about. They were standing for quite a while right outside the door to the miller's private room. I was lying at their feet, but they'd neither eyes nor thoughts for me. "I'm going straight in to your father!" said Rudy, "it's a just cause." "Shall I come with you?" said Babette, "it'll give you courage!" "I've plenty enough courage of my own," said Rudy, "but if you were with me, he'd have to look kindly on us whether he wants to or not."

'And so they went in, Rudy stepping on me very heavily in the hall; Rudy can be unspeakably clumsy. I miaowed, but neither he nor Babette had ears to hear me. They opened the door, the two of them went inside, with me going in front. But I jumped up onto the back of a chair, I couldn't know whether Rudy would be giving out kicks of some kind. But it was the miller who did the kicking. It was a terrific kick too. Out through the door and up into the mountains with the chamois! It's *them* Rudy has to aim at now, and not our little Babette.'

'But what was actually said?' asked the Kitchen Cat.

'*Said!* – Everything was said, the sort of things people say when they're proposing marriage. "I'm fond of her, and she's fond of me!" And "When there's milk in the churn for one, there's also milk in the churn for two!"

'"But she has a very high position socially," the miller said, "she's right up there with my grain, my golden grain. You know perfectly well you don't come anywhere near her!"

'"But nothing's too high up to reach when you've a mind to!" said Rudy, for he's very quick on the draw.

'"Well, the eaglet – you can't reach *him*; you admitted as much when you were here last. And Babette's position is higher still."

'"I'm going to get both of them!" said Rudy.

'"All right, I'll make you a present of her when you've made me a present of the young eagle *alive*," said the miller, and laughed so that tears streamed down his face. "But thanks very much for your visit, Rudy! Come again tomorrow morning, and you'll find nobody at home. Goodbye, Rudy!"

'And Babette said goodbye too, as pathetic as a little kitten who can't see her mother. "When a man's a man his word's his word!" said Rudy. "Don't cry, Babette, I'll bring you the eaglet."

'"You'll break your neck, I hope!" said the miller, "and then we'll have got you well and truly out of the way!"

'That's what I call a thorough kicking. Rudy has now taken himself off, and Babette is sitting and sobbing, but the miller is singing a German song that he's learned on his travels. I won't grieve over it all, it wouldn't help.'

'But it's always good to give a show of doing so,' said the Kitchen Cat.

7. The eagle's nest

From the mountain path the yodelling rang out so merry and full-bodied it suggested high spirits and intrepid courage. It was Rudy; he'd gone to see his friend Vesinand.

'You have to help me! We'll take Ragli along too. I've got to get hold of the young eagle up on the mountain edge.'

'Wouldn't you like to get hold of the dark side of the moon first? It's every bit as easy!' said Vesinand. 'You seem in a very good mood, Rudy!'

'Yes, because I'm thinking of getting married. But right now, speaking seriously, you'd better know how matters stand with me.'

And soon Vesinand and Ragli knew what it was that Rudy wanted.

'You're a real daredevil!' they said, 'it won't work! You'll break your neck!'

'You don't fall when you don't think you're going to,' said Rudy.

Towards midnight they set off, taking with them poles, ladders and rope. Their route led between thickets and bushes, across crumbly stones, always upwards, up into the dark night. Down below the water roared, up above the water murmured, rain-clouds drifted through the air. The hunters reached the precipitous mountain edge. It became darker here; the mountain-walls all but met at this point, and only high up, through the narrow crack between them, did the sky show any light at all. Close by, beneath the three young men, was a deep abyss full of torrential water. All three sat there motionless. They'd wait for dawn, when the adult eagle would fly out. She had to be shot first, before there could be any notion of taking the young one. Rudy squatted as still as if he were a portion of the stone he was sitting on. He had his gun in front of him, poised to shoot, his eyes intently on the furthermost cleft where, inside, under the overhanging cliff, the eagle's nest was hidden. The three hunters waited for a long time.

Now, high above them, came a whizzing, rushing noise. A huge object hovering overhead intensified the darkness. Two gun-barrels took aim as the black eagle-shape flew out of the nest. One shot was fired. For a moment the outstretched wings flapped, and then slowly the bird went down. With its vast body-dimensions and its great wingspan it would surely fill the entire ravine, and in its fall sweep the hunters away. But the eagle sank into the abyss; there was a groaning in the tree-branches and bushes which were broken by the bird's fall.

And now hectic activity began. Three of the longest ladders were tied together; they had to reach the top. The ladders were set in place on the outermost, last foothold on the edge of the precipice, but they did not reach the top; and the long stretch of cliff higher up, where the nest was hidden in the lee of the furthest jutting protrusion of rock, was as smooth as any ordinary house-wall. After some deliberation the young men agreed they couldn't do better than to hoist from above two ladders tied together down into the ravine, and then connect these to the three that had already been positioned from below. With great difficulty they dragged the two ladders further up, and there made the ropes fast. Then the ladders were pushed out over the overhanging cliff and so hung freely over the chasm; Rudy was already sitting there on the lowest rung. It was a freezing cold morning, the cloudy mist was drifting downwards from the black cleft. Rudy sat out there like a fly sitting on the bobbing straw that some nest-building bird has dropped on the rim of a tall factory-chimney. But the fly can fly away when the straw begins to slacken, Rudy could only break his neck. The wind was whistling round him, and down in the abyss the hurry-scurrying water roared out from the thaw-beset glacier, the Ice Virgin's palace.

Now he set the ladder in a swinging movement, like a spider's web which by means of its long, stretching thread can grip tightly, and when Rudy, at the fourth attempt, touched the tip of the ladders that had been put in place from below and tied together, he got a good hold of them. They were then joined up with strong, confident hands, though they continued to swing as though on worn-out hinges.

The five long ladders now seemed like one long swaying bamboo plant which, leaning against the rock-wall perpendicularly, reached up very close to the eagle's nest. Now, though, came the most dangerous part: having to crawl as the cat crawls. But Rudy knew how to do this; the tomcat had taught him. He didn't even feel Her Dizziness treading the air behind him, and stretching out her polyp's arms after him. He was now standing on the ladder's topmost rung, and noticed that even here he hadn't got up high enough to see inside the nest. He could reach it with his hand only. He tested how firm its lowest part was, the thick branches woven together which formed the bottom of the nest. And when he had got secure hold of a stout, trustworthy branch, he swung himself up off the ladder, his body against the branch, until he had his torso and head over the nest itself.

But here a suffocating stench of carrion streamed forth to greet him. Putrescent lambs, chamois and birds lay here dismembered. Her Dizziness, who had not as yet been strong enough to affect him, blew the noxious vapours in his face for him to go giddy, and fall down into the black, gaping deep, into the furious water on which the Ice Virgin herself was sitting, with her long white-green hair, staring with dead eyes like two gun-barrels.

'Now I'll take you captive!'

In a corner of the eagle's nest Rudy saw sitting, large and powerful, the young eagle who was as yet unable to fly. Rudy fixed his eyes on him, held himself with one hand as strongly as he could, and then with his other hand threw a noose round the eaglet. The bird was captured very much alive, his legs caught in the ever-tightening cord. And Rudy slung the noose with the bird in it over his shoulder so that the creature could dangle a good way below him, as now, with the aid of a lowered rope, he held on fast till the tips of his feet gained the topmost rung of the ladder once more.

'Hold tight. Don't think you're going to fall, and fall you won't!' It was the old piece of wisdom, and he followed it. Held on tightly, then crawled, was convinced he wouldn't fall, and fall he did not.

Now a great yodel burst out, very strong and cheery. Rudy was standing on firm rocky ground with his young eagle.

8. What the Parlour Cat had to tell

'Here's what you asked for!' said Rudy, coming into the miller's house in Bex and putting a large cage down on the floor. He removed the cloth covering it, and two yellow, black-encircled eyes glared out, so brilliant and so savage, as if eager to burn and take hold wherever they looked. The short, strong beak was opening to bite, the neck was red and downy.

'The eaglet!' the miller exclaimed. Babette gave a scream and jumped to one side, but she could not keep her eyes either from Rudy or from the young eagle.

'Well, you didn't let yourself get scared!' said the miller.

'And you're somebody who always keeps his word,' said Rudy, 'everyone's got his own special characteristic!'

'But how come you didn't break your neck?' asked the miller.

'Because I held on tight,' replied Rudy, 'and that's what I'm still doing. I'm holding on tight to Babette.'

'Why don't you see first whether you've got her!' said the miller, and laughed, and that was a good sign, Babette knew.

'Let's take the young eagle out of his cage. It's dangerous just to look at the way he glowers! However did you catch him?"

And Rudy had to tell the story, and the miller's eyes got bigger and bigger as he did so.

'With your guts and your good luck you could provide for *three* wives,' said the miller.

'Thank you, thanks a lot!' exclaimed Rudy.

'Yes, but you still don't have Babette yet,' said the miller, and he clapped Rudy on the shoulder in jest.

'Do you know the news from the mill?' said the Parlour Cat to the Kitchen Cat, 'Rudy's brought us a young eagle, and is now taking Babette in exchange. They've kissed one another, and in front of Father! It's as good as an engagement. The Old Man didn't do any kicking, he's drawn in his claws, and has now taken an after-dinner nap and left the two of them to sit and spoon. They have such a lot to talk about, they won't be through by Christmas.'

And they weren't through by Christmas! The wind whirled the brown leaves, the snow drifted into the valley from the high mountains. The Ice Virgin sat in her splendid palace, which expands in size in winter-time. The rock-walls stood with black ice coating and icicles thick as your arm and as heavy as an elephant, there where in summer the mountain stream waves its watery veils. Ice garlands formed by fantastic crystals shone above the snow-powdered spruce trees.

The Ice Virgin went riding on the tearing wind across the deepest valleys. The carpet of snow stretched out all the way down to Bex. She was able to come and peer in on Rudy who was indoors far more than he was ever used to being; he was making himself at home at Babette's. The wedding would take place in the summer. So frequently did their friends talk about it that the pair's ears would often be buzzing. Sunshine came, the loveliest Alpine rose glowed, that is to say the happy, laughing Babette herself, delightful as the spring, which duly arrived, spring which made all the birds sing till summer-time about the wedding-day.

'How can the two of them just sit there and breathe down each other's necks!' said the Parlour Cat, 'I'm even bored with miaowing now!'

9. The Ice Virgin

Spring had brought out its lush green festoon of walnut and chestnut trees. It was especially profuse, from the bridge at St Maurice to Lake Geneva, all along the Rhône, which shot forth with tremendous speed from its source, the green glacier, the Ice Palace where the Ice Virgin lives. From here she lets the keen wind carry her up to the most distant snowfield to stretch out in the strong sunlight on snowdrift bolsters. There she sat and looked with far-distance vision down into the deep valley, where human beings, like ants on a sun-kissed stone, were busily at work.

'Powers of the Mind! – as the Children of the Sun call you!' said the Ice Virgin, 'you're vermin! One rolling snowball of mine, and you and your houses and towns are crushed and obliterated!' And she raised her proud head higher and looked far and wide and deep downwards with her death-dealing eyes. But from the valley a great rumbling sounded, an explosion of rocks, human activity: the tracks and tunnels for the railway were under construction.

'They're playing at being moles!' she said, 'they're digging passageways; that's why you hear a noise like gunshots. Whereas when I move my castle, you hear a roaring greater even than thunderbolts.'

From the valley a column of smoke rose up. It moved forwards like a fluttering veil, a waving plume, from the engine which, down on the newly-opened railway, was pulling the train, this winding snake whose joints were carriages linked to one another. Like an arrow it shot ahead.

'The Powers of the Mind are playing at being lords-and-masters!' said the Ice Virgin, 'however, the powers of Nature's forces are the ones getting their way.' And she laughed and she sang, the sound ringing out in the valley.

'There was an avalanche rolling up there just now!' said the men down below.

But higher up still the Children of the Sun were singing about human thought, which *does* get its way, which can harness the sea, move mountains, fill valleys, human thought which is lord-and-master of Nature's powers. At the very same moment, over the snowfield where the Ice Virgin was sitting, a bunch of travellers came along. They had tied green veils over their faces so the snow's white glare wouldn't burn them. They had tied themselves fast to one another, to resemble one single big body on the slippery sheets of ice by the deep abyss.

'Vermin!' she said again, '*you* to be lords-and-masters over the power of Nature!' And she turned herself round and looked mockingly down into the deep valley where the railway train roared past.

'There they sit, these *thoughts*! They're just targets for the violence of our forces! I see every one of them! One is sitting proud as a king, alone! The others sit all in a huddle, half of them asleep! And when the steam-dragon comes to a halt, out they climb, going on their way. The *thoughts* are going out into the world.' And she laughed.

'That was another avalanche rolling!' they said down in the valley.

'But nowhere near us!' said two people on the back of the steam-dragon, 'two souls and one mind', as they say. It was Rudy and Babette; the miller was with them too.

'Like luggage,' he said, 'I'm there because it's necessary.'

'There the two of them sit!' said the Ice Virgin, 'I've crushed many chamois, and I've smashed and destroyed millions of Alpine roses, with not so much as a root left. I wipe them all out. Thoughts! Powers of the Mind!' And she laughed.

'That was yet another avalanche!' they said down in the valley.

10. Godmother

Babette's godmother was staying, with her daughters and a young kinsman, in Montreux, for visitors from Bex one of the nearest towns that form, together with Clarens, Vernex and Crin, a garland round Lake Geneva's north-eastern corner. They were newly ensconced there, yet the miller had already paid them a visit, and relayed Babette's engagement, telling them about Rudy and the eaglet, and the visit to Interlaken, telling them in short the whole story. And they were delighted by it and consumed with interest in Rudy and Babette, and in the miller as well. They absolutely must, all three of them, come on over, and therefore come on over they did. Babette would see her godmother, her godmother would see Babette.

The steamer which takes half-an-hour to reach Vernex, immediately below Montreux, was docked at the little town of Villeneuve, at the extreme eastern end of Lake Geneva. This shoreline is more celebrated in literature than almost any other. Here, beneath the walnut trees, beside the deep blue-green lake, Byron sat and wrote his melodious verses about the prisoner in the sinister fortress of Chillon. Over there, where Clarens with its weeping willows is reflected in the water, Rousseau wandered dreaming about Heloïse. The River Rhône glides forth beneath the Savoy's high, snow-clad mountains, and here, at no great distance from its outlet into the lake, lies a little island. It's so small that from the shore you could well fancy it was a boat out there. It is a piece of rocky ground which a hundred years earlier its mistress decided should be dyked with stones, covered with soil, and planted with three acacia trees. These now overshadow the whole island. Babette was altogether thrilled by this little spot. For her it was the most beautiful part of the entire boat trip. They really should get out onto it, they simply *must* go onto it; being there would be beautiful beyond words, she thought. But the steamer went on past and set them down, as programmed, at Vernex.

From here the little company strolled uphill between the white, sunlit walls that surround the vineyards immediately below the little mountain town of Montreux, where fig trees cast shadows in front of the smallholders' houses, and laurels and cypresses grow in the gardens. Halfway up the hill stood the *pension* where Godmother was staying.

Their reception was cordial in the extreme. Godmother was a friendly old lady, with a round, smiling face. As a child she must have been a truly Raphaelesque cherub, but now she had a venerable cherub-head all beset by silvery-white curly hair. Her daughters were well turned out, fashion-conscious, tall and slim. The young male cousin who was with them and who was dressed entirely in white from top to toe, with gilded hair and gilded sideburns so profuse they could have been shared out among three gentlemen, gave little Babette his utmost attention from the very start.

Handsome clothbound books, sheets of music and drawings all lay spread out on top of the large table. The balcony door stood open to the beautiful lake that stretched out in front so bright and calm that the Savoy Mountains with their villages, forests and snow-peaks were mirrored in it upside down.

Rudy, who in other circumstances was always bold, lively and confident, felt not in the least at his ease, as people call it. He moved about here as if he were walking on peas across a slippery floor. How hard it was to get through the time! It was like being on a treadmill – and now it was decided they should all go for a walk!! That went by so slowly. Two steps forwards and one step back was how Rudy managed to keep the same pace as the others.

They all went down to Chillon, the grim castle on the rocky island, to look at torture instruments and condemned cells, at rusty chains attached to the rock-wall, stone beds for those on death row, trapdoors through which the unfortunate were pushed down to be impaled on iron spikes sticking up from the lake-surf. And they called looking at all this a *pleasure*! It was a place of execution elevated by Byron's song into the world of poetry. But for Rudy it was merely a place of execution. He leaned out of the window's large stone frame, gazing down into the deep, blue-green water and then across to the beautiful little island with the three acacias, where he wished he were by himself, free of this whole chattering company. But Babette was feeling extremely happy. She had enjoyed herself enormously, she said later; she found the English cousin 'perfect'.

'Yes, a perfect nincompoop!' said Rudy, and that was the first time Rudy had said anything that did not please her. The young Englishman had made her a present of a little book as a memento of Chillon. It was Byron's poem *The Prisoner of Chillon* translated into French so Babette could read it.

'The book might be good enough,' said Rudy, 'but personally I don't take to the smart-combed dandy who gave you it at all.'

'He looks like a sack of flour without the flour!' said the miller and laughed at his own wit. Rudy laughed too, and said a truer word was never spoken.

11. The cousin

When a couple of days later Rudy paid a visit to the mill, he found the young Englishman there. Babette was setting some boiled trout in front of him. She had obviously decorated them with parsley herself to give them an elegant appearance. That was not at all necessary! Whatever did the Englishman want here? What would he be up to in this place? Having Babette play with him and run rings round him?

Rudy was jealous, and that amused Babette. It entertained her to observe all aspects of his heart, the strong and the weak. Love was still a game, and she was playing with the entirety of Rudy's heart, and yet, it should be said, he was her joy, her life's ideal, the best, the most wonderful in this world. But the gloomier he looked, the more her eyes laughed. She would have liked to have kissed the fair Englishman with the gilded sideburns. If by doing so she made Rudy run away in fury, that would just go to show how hugely he adored her. Yet that was neither right nor wise of little Babette, but then she was only nineteen. She didn't think things through, even less did she think how her behaviour could be interpreted by the young Englishman as more flirtatious and easy-going than was quite proper for the miller's modest, newly engaged daughter.

Where the highway from Bex runs below the snow-covered rocky height which is called in the language of the region Les Diablerets, the mill stood, at no great distance from a fast-flowing mountain stream which was whitish-grey in colour like whipped-up soapy water. This however was not what drove the mill. It was a smaller stream that did so, which tumbled down from the rock on the other side of the river, and subsequently, by its power and speed, elevated itself through a stone underground duct beneath the road and then flowed into a closed tank. Thus a wide race running *above* the fast-flowing river turned the great mill-wheel.

The race was so abundantly full of water it was overflowing, and accordingly presented a wet and filthy route to anyone with the notion of using it as a quick way of getting to the mill-house. But that indeed was the notion of one young man, the Englishman. Dressed in white like a miller's journeyman, he scrambled along it in the evening, guided by the light that shone from Babette's bedroom. Having never learned to clamber or climb, he nearly went head-first into the stream, but escaped with wet sleeves and mud-bespattered trousers. Drenched and dirty, he arrived below one of Babette's windows, from which position he climbed up onto the old lime tree and there mimicked the owl, not being able to render the call of any other bird. Babette heard it and peeked out through the thin curtains of her room, but when she saw the white man and realised who it was, her little heart beat with fear, but also with rage. She quickly extinguished her light, made sure the windows were securely bolted, and just let him get on with his tu-whit-tu-whooing.

How dreadful it would be if Rudy were here now at the mill. But Rudy was *not* at the mill; no, it was far worse, he was actually right down there below. Furious words were shouted out loudly; a fight would break out, there might possibly be a murder.

Babette opened her window in terror, called out Rudy's name, and bade him go away. She couldn't bear him to stay, she said.

'You can't bear me to stay!' he exclaimed, 'it's obviously an assignation. You're waiting for fine friends, better than me! Shame on you, Babette!'

'You're detestable!' said Babette, 'I hate you!' and now she was weeping. 'Go on, go away!'

'I don't deserve this,' he said, and he left, cheeks afire, heart afire.

Babette threw herself on her bed and wept.

'I love you so much, Rudy, yet you're able to believe ill of me!'

And she was angry, exceedingly angry, and that was good for her, otherwise she would have been completely overcome by distress. As it was, she was able to fall asleep, and sleep the refreshing sleep of youth.

12. Evil powers

Rudy left Bex for home, taking the high mountain route for the sake of the fresh, cooling air – up where the snow lay, where the Ice Virgin reigned. The deciduous trees stood far below as if they were mere potato-tops, fir and shrubs became smaller in size, the Alpine roses grew close to the snow which lay in isolated patches like pieces of linen being bleached. A single blue gentian stood its ground; Rudy smashed it with his rifle.

Higher up two chamois came in sight. Rudy's eyes lit up, his thoughts took off in a new direction. But he was not near enough to take an accurate shot. He climbed higher still, to where only a rough type of grass was growing between the boulders. The chamois went in peace onto the snowfield. Rudy hurried along eagerly. The cloud banks were getting lower all round him, and all of a sudden he found himself in front of a precipitous rock-wall just as the rain began to pour down.

He felt a scorching thirst, heat in his head and coldness in his other limbs. He grasped his hunter's flask, but it was empty; he hadn't thought of that when he charged up into the mountains. He had never been ill, but now he had a kind of taste of what it was like. He was done in, he felt a longing to fling himself down and go to sleep, but everything was streaming with water. He tried to pull himself together. Objects were quivering most peculiarly before his eyes, but suddenly he saw what he had never seen here before, a little house recently carpentered together and leaning against the rock-wall. And in the doorway stood a young girl. He thought it was the schoolmaster's Annette whom he had once kissed at the dance, but it was not Annette, and yet he had seen her before, possibly near Grindelwald that evening he'd made his way home from the shooting contest at Interlaken.

'However have you got here?' he asked.

'I'm at my home,' she said, 'I'm looking after my herd.'

'Your *herd* – and where does it graze? Up here's only snow and rocks.'

'What a lot you know!' she said, laughing. 'Below the surface here, only a little way down, there's delicious grass. That's where my goats go! I never lose a single one of them. What's mine stays mine!'

'You're a bold one!' said Rudy.

'You are too!' she replied.

'If you've got any milk, spare me some! I'm intolerably thirsty.'

'I've got something better than milk,' she said, 'and you shall have some of it. Yesterday some travellers came up here with their guides. They left behind half a flask of wine the like of which you'll never ever have tasted. *They* are not coming back for it, *I* am not going to drink it – so *you've* got to drink it!'

And she brought out the wine, poured it into a wooden cup and gave it to Rudy.

'It's good!' he said, 'I've never tasted such warming, such fiery wine!' And his eyes sparkled. A renewal of life, a glow came over him, as if sorrows and burdens were evaporating. Bubbling, vital human nature was stirring in him.

'But it really must be the schoolmaster's Annette!' he exclaimed. 'Give me a kiss!'

'Yes, all right, but give me the beautiful ring you're wearing on your finger!'

'My engagement ring?'

'Exactly that!' said the girl, pouring wine into the wooden cup and putting it to his lips, and he drank. Happiness in being alive coursed through his blood; the whole world was his, he felt, why worry oneself further? Everything exists for our enjoyment and to make us happy. The stream of life is the stream of happiness. To be carried along by it, to permit oneself to be carried along by it, that is what bliss means. Rudy looked at the young girl; it was Annette and yet it was not Annette, still less was it the troll apparition, as he'd called her, whom he'd encountered near Grindelwald. The girl on the mountain here was as pure as new-fallen snow, full as an Alpine rose, and light as a young chamois, yet basically made from Adam's rib, as human as Rudy. And he flung his arms round her, and gazed into her wondrous clear eyes. It was only for a second, and in this time – yes, explain it, make a narrative of it, put it into words for us all – was it the life of the spirit or of death that filled him? Was he raised up or did he sink down into the deep, deadly ice chasm, deeper, ever deeper?

He saw walls of ice like blue-green glass; endless gullies opened all round him, and the water drip-dropped ringing out like a carillon, and yet also clear as pearls shining in blue-white flames. The Ice Virgin gave him a kiss, which made him shiver through every bone in his head. He gave a cry of pain, wrenched himself free, stumbled and fell. It became night before his eyes, yet open them again he did. Evil powers had come to the end of their game.

The Alpine girl had vanished, gone away from the hut that had been sheltering her. Water streamed down the bare rock-wall, snow lay all round, Rudy was shaking with cold, soaked to the skin – and his ring had disappeared, the engagement ring Babette had given him. His rifle lay in the snow beside him; he picked it up and tried to shoot from it, but misfired. Rain-clouds lay inside the ravine like firm masses of snow. Her Dizziness was sitting there, enticing guileless prey, and beneath her there came a ringing noise in the chasm as if a boulder were falling, crushing and annihilating whatever stood in the way of its descent.

But in the mill Babette sat and wept. Rudy had not been there for six days. He who had done her such an injustice, he who should be extending both hands for forgiveness, because she loved him with all her heart.

13. In the miller's house

'There's an awful lot of nonsense going on among the human beings!' said the Parlour Cat to the Kitchen Cat. 'Babette and Rudy have broken things off *yet* again. She's weeping away, and he isn't thinking of her any more.'

'I don't like that at all!' said the Kitchen Cat.

'I don't either!' said the Parlour Cat, 'but I'm not going to grieve over it. Babette can go and become the loved one of that carroty sideburns fellow. He hasn't been here either, not since he had a mind to go out onto the roof!'

Evil powers have their game, all round us and within us. Rudy had realised that, and thought it over. What was it that happened round him and inside him high up on the mountain? Was it visions or a dream in a fever? – he'd never known fever or illness before. He'd gained an insight into himself even as he passed judgement on Babette. He thought about the ferocious chase that had broken out in his own heart, the torrid Föhn that had been released there. Would he find himself able to confess everything to Babette, every idea that in a moment of temptation could turn into action? He had lost her ring, and it was precisely through this loss she had got him back. But would *she* be able to confess to *him*? It was as though, as he thought about her, his heart was on the point of breaking into pieces. So many memories asserted themselves. He saw her full of life, laughing, a high-spirited child. Many a loving word that she had spoken out of the fullness of her heart flew like a ray of sun into his breast, and before long real sunshine prevailed there for Babette.

She had to find the ability to confess to him, and that she should do.

He turned up at the mill. The result was a confession which began with a kiss and ended with Rudy being the sinner. His great error was being capable of actually doubting Babette's faithfulness. It was, well, *detestable* of him! Such lack of trust, such impetuosity would lead them both to misery. Yes, most definitely it would! And that was why Babette preached him a little sermon, which she found very pleasing to deliver and which made her look so pretty. Yet in one respect (she conceded) Rudy had a point. Her godmother's kinsman was a nincompoop! She would burn the book he had given her, and wouldn't keep the smallest thing to remind her of him.

'Now it's all over and done with!' said the Parlour Cat. 'Rudy is here again, they understand each other, and that's the greatest happiness of all, they say.'

'Last night,' said the Kitchen Cat, 'I heard the rats say the greatest happiness comes from eating tallow-candles and bloating yourself with rotten pork. Now which should you believe, rats or people in love?'

'None of them!' said the Parlour Cat. 'That's always safest!'

The greatest happiness for Rudy and Babette was in fact growing. Their finest day, as people call it, they now had in sight, their wedding day.

But the wedding would not be taking place in the church at Bex, nor in the miller's house. Babette's godmother wanted the wedding celebrated at her place, and the marriage ceremony to be conducted in the beautiful little church in Montreux. The miller insisted this request was granted. He alone knew what Godmother had arranged for the newly-weds; they were getting a wedding present well worth such a modest compliance. The day was decided on. Already the evening beforehand they would have made their way to Villeneuve before setting off by steamer in the morning for Montreux so Godmother's daughters could deck the bride.

'There'll be a two-days-long wedding-feast in this house too!' said the Parlour Cat, 'otherwise I think the whole thing won't be worth so much as a miaow!'

'The feast's in progress right here,' said the Kitchen Cat, 'the ducks have been killed, the pigeons have had their necks wrung, and a whole deer carcass is hanging up on the wall. I'd give my teeth and claws to witness it all. Tomorrow they're starting on their journey!'

Yes, the next day. This evening Rudy and Babette sat in the mill-house for the last time as an affianced couple.

Outside was the alpenglow, the evening bell rang out, and the daughters of the sunbeams sang: 'May what's best be what happens!'

14. Visions in the night

The sun was down; in the Rhône Valley between the high mountains the clouds were descending. The wind, a wind from Africa, blew from the south across the high Alps, a Föhn which tore the clouds into shreds. And when the wind had raced off, for just a moment it became completely calm. Between the forest-covered mountains across the scurrying River Rhône the fragmented clouds hung in fantastic shapes. They hung in shapes like sea-monsters from the prehistoric world, like eagles hovering in the air, like jumping frogs from the marsh. They descended onto the fast-coursing stream, sailing on it and sailing in the air as well. The stream carried an upturned branch complete with root; the water in front of this resembled revolving whirlpools. That was Her Dizziness, in more than one manifestation, turning the rapid stream round and round. The moon was shining on the snow of the mountain-tops, on the dark forests and the mysterious white clouds, visions of the night, the souls of Nature's forces. The mountain peasant looked at them through a window-pane; they were sailing downwards in flocks before the Ice Virgin. She arrived from her glacier palace, sitting on that fragile vessel, the upturned branch, water from the glacier bearing her down the stream to the open lake.

'The wedding-guests are coming!' That's what was being whispered and sung in the air and the water.

Visions without, visions within. Babette dreamed an extraordinary dream.

It seemed to her as if she were married to Rudy, already had been so for many years. Right now he was away on a chamois-hunt, but she was at home, and there sitting by her side was the young Englishman with the gilded sideburns. His eyes were so ardent, his words had the power of an enchantment. He reached out a hand to her, and she simply had to follow him. They went a long way from her home. Constantly downwards! – and against her heart Babette felt a weight that became heavier and heavier. It was a sin against Rudy, a sin against God. And all of a sudden she was standing abandoned, her clothes torn into shreds by the white-thorn. Her hair was grey. She looked up, and on the mountain edge she spied Rudy. She stretched out her arms towards him, but didn't dare call out or entreat him, and anyway it wouldn't have done any good, because she soon saw that it wasn't him but his hunting jacket and hat that hung on an alpenstock such as the hunters put out to fool the chamois. And in immeasurable anguish Babette moaned: 'If only I'd died on my wedding-day, on my happiest day. My Lord, my God, it would have been a mercy, a whole life's crowning joy. Then what's for the best would have happened, the best that could happen for me and Rudy! Nobody knows the future!' And in the agony of unbelief, she hurled herself down into the mountain chasm. A string as of an instrument snapped, a note of lamentation rang out.

Babette woke up, the dream was at an end – and was erased, but she knew she had dreamed something appalling, and dreamed about the young Englishman whom she hadn't seen in several months and not even thought about. Was he, she wondered, in Montreux? Would she get to see him at the wedding? A little shadow flitted across her delicate mouth. Her brows puckered, but soon a smile appeared on her face, and her eyes blinked; the sun was shining outside so beautifully, and tomorrow was her and Rudy's wedding-day.

He was in the parlour already when she came downstairs, and presently they made their way to Villeneuve. The two of them were so happy, and the miller as well; he laughed and beamed in the most benevolent humour, a good father, an honest soul.

'Now we have a Master-and-Mistress for our home!' said the Parlour Cat.

15. The end

It was not yet evening when the three happy people reached Villeneuve and had their meal. The miller sat himself in an easy chair with his pipe and took a little nap. The young betrothed went arm-in-arm into the town, along the carriage-road beneath the shrub-covered rocks beside the deep blue-green lake. Grim Chillon had its grey walls and doughty towers reflected in the clear water. The little island with the three acacia trees lay closer still; it resembled a bouquet of flowers tossed onto the lake.

'It must be beautiful over there!' said Babette. Once again she felt the greatest desire to go across to it, and as it happened that wish could be instantly made good. A boat lay by the bank, the chain that moored it was easy enough to undo. Nobody was in sight to ask permission from, and so they took over the boat without anyone knowing. Rudy was a competent rower.

The oars moved like a fish's fins in the compliant water.

Water is both so pliable and so strong; it has a back for carrying, it has a mouth for swallowing which sometimes smiles gently, with even a softness about it, and yet is also alarming and powerful enough to smash things to bits. A foaming wake followed the boat, which with the two of them in it took only a few minutes to reach the island where they clambered ashore. Here there was no more room than for just one dance for the two of them.

Rudy swung Babette round two or three times, and then they went and sat down on the little bench beneath the drooping acacias, gazing into each other's eyes, holding each other's hands, while everything in the vicinity shone in the radiance of the setting sun. The spruce forests on the mountains acquired a mauve appearance, very much like heather in bloom, and where the trees left off and the rock protruded, it was glowing as if the mountain were transparent. The clouds in the sky were like red fire, the entire lake suggested a fresh, blushing rose-petal. The shadows, one and all, stole upwards towards the snow-clad mountains of the Savoy; these turned blue-black, but the highest peak of all maintained the shine of red lava. They witnessed anew a moment from the mountains' very formation, when these glowing masses rose out of earth's womb and had not yet been extinguished. It was an alpenglow such as Rudy and Babette had never believed they would see the like of. The snow-decked Dents du Midi had a sheen like the face of the full moon when it ascends from the horizon.

'So much beauty, so much joy!' the couple said. 'Earth can't give me anything more!' said Rudy, 'One evening hour like this is a lifetime in itself! How often I've felt happiness, just like I'm feeling now, and thought that if everything was about to end, then how happy my life has been, how full of blessings this world is! – and then the day would come to its end, but a new one would begin in its place, and that, it'd seem to me, was even more beautiful. Our Father is infinitely good, Babette!'

'I'm so very happy!' she said.

'Earth can't give me anything more!' Rudy pronounced again.

And the evening bells rang out from the mountains of the Savoy, from the mountains of Switzerland. Against the golden glory of sunset the blue-black Jura rose against the west.

'May God give you whatever's most wonderful, whatever's truly best!' exclaimed Babette.

'That's what He is going to do!' said Rudy. 'Tomorrow that's what I'll be having! Tomorrow you will be completely mine! My own beautiful little wife!'

'The boat!' Babette cried out at that very moment.

The boat, which was their means of getting back, had got loose from its moorings and was drifting away from the island.

'I'll go and fetch it!' said Rudy, and he took off his coat, pulled off his boots, leaped into the lake, and made off with rapid strokes in the direction of the boat.

Cold and deep was the clear, blue-green ice-water from the mountain glacier. Rudy looked down into it, only one single glance, and it was as though he saw a gold ring rolling, gleaming, jiggling – the engagement ring he had lost and thought such a lot about, and the ring was getting larger, expanding into a glittering circle, inside which shone the limpid glacier. Countless deep chasms gaped all round, and the water was falling with the chiming sound of a glockenspiel, and shining with blue-white flames. In the twinkling of an eye Rudy saw what we are obliged to use many long words to convey. Young huntsmen and young girls, men and women who had at one time or another vanished into the clefts of the glacier, were standing here with open eyes and smiling mouths, and far below them there pealed the ringing of church bells from submerged towns. The congregation was kneeling under the church vaults, the icicles formed organ-pipes, the mountain stream provided the organ. The Ice Virgin herself sat on the clear transparent floor. She raised herself up to get at Rudy, kissed his feet, and through his limbs passed a deathly shudder, an electric shock! Ice and fire, you can't make a distinction between them just from brief contact.

'Mine! Mine!' It resounded all around him, and inside him too. 'I kissed you when you were little, kissed you on the mouth. Now I kiss you on your toe and your heel, and the whole of you is mine.'

And he disappeared into the clear blue water.

Everything was quiet; the church bells left off ringing, the last notes dying down with the radiance of the red clouds.

'You are mine!' That rang out in the depths. 'You are mine!' and that rang out into the heights, a message from eternity.

Bliss to fly from love to love, from earth into heaven! A string snapped, a note of lamentation resonated. Death's kiss of ice had overcome the corruptible flesh. The prelude had ended before the drama of life had been able to begin. The discord was dissolved in harmony.

Would you call that a sorrowful story?

Poor Babette, for her it was an hour of agony! The boat drifted further and further away. Nobody on the mainland knew that the bridal couple were on the island. Evening came on; the clouds descended; darkness arrived. She remained there, alone, in despair, moaning, wailing. The play of the elements went on overhead. Lightning flashed across the mountains of the Jura, across Switzerland and the Savoy. From all sides, flash after flash, boom upon boom succeeded one another, each several minutes long. The lightning flashes soon acquired the brightness of the sun, every single vine could be seen just as if it were midday, and then black darkness swamped everything again. The lightning streaks formed loops, conductors for other types of light, and in zigzags struck all round the lake. From every side they were brilliant, while the booms grew louder with the rumble of their echo. Back on land they were dragging the boats up onto the beach. Everything that was still alive was seeking shelter – and now the rain came pouring down.

'Wherever can Rudy and Babette be in this fearful storm!' said the miller. Babette was sitting with hands clasped, with her head in her lap, dumb with anguish, incapable of screaming or wailing.

'In the deep water,' she said to herself, 'he's far down below, way beneath the glacier.'

Into her thoughts came what Rudy had told her about his mother's death and his rescue when he had been hauled up out of the glacier's chasms, thought to be a corpse himself. 'The Ice Virgin has him again.'

And a stroke of lightning shone so dazzlingly, like the glare of sun on white snow. Babette ran backwards and forwards in the storm. Simultaneously the lake rose like a shimmering glacier; the Ice Virgin was standing there, regal, pale blue, aglow, and at her feet lay Rudy's dead body. 'Mine!' she said, and again it was pitch darkness and rushing water all around.

'How cruel everything is,' lamented Babette. 'Why should he have to die, just as our day of happiness was at hand? God, grant me light for my mind, God, give me light for my heart! I don't understand your ways. I'm just fumbling about faced with your almighty power and wisdom.'

And God listened to her heart. Like an inspiration, a ray of mercy, her dream of the previous night sped through her. She recollected the words she had uttered; her wish for the best possible thing to happen to herself and Rudy.

'Help me! It was the seeds of sin in my heart. My dream was a portent of future life, and its string had to be cut for the sake of saving my soul. Wretch that I am!'

In its profound stillness there rang out, it seemed to her, Rudy's words: 'Earth can't give me any happiness more!' They had rung out in the fullness of happiness, they were now repeated in the torrent of misery.

A couple of years have gone by since then. The lake is smiling, its shores are smiling too. The vine is putting forth grapes; the steamers with their fluttering flags chug their way forwards; yachts with their pairs of outstretched sails fly like white butterflies across the mirror-like water. The railway line beyond Chillon is open now; it leads deep into the Rhône Valley. At every station foreigners get out, they arrive with their red-bound guidebook and read what noteworthy sight they should look at. They visit Chillon; out there in the lake they see the tiny island with the three acacias and read in their book about the bride and bridegroom who sailed over there one evening in the year 1856, about the bridegroom's death and how 'first thing the next morning the heartbroken cries of the bride were heard on the shore.'

But the travel-book mentions nothing of Babette's peaceful daily life with her father, not at the mill where strangers live now, but in a charming house near the railway station, where many an evening she looks across from the window, over the chestnut trees, to the snow-mountains where Rudy used to run about. And at the appropriate evening hour she watches the alpenglow. The children of the sun still make encampment up there and sing again the song of the wanderer whose cap the whirlwind took off and carried away, removing the covering but not the essential man.

There is roseate radiance on the mountain's snows, there is roseate radiance in every heart that contains the idea: 'God lets the best for us happen!' But that isn't always made manifest to us in quite the way it was for Babette in her dream.

AFTERWORD

'LET'S VISIT SWITZERLAND,' Hans Christian Andersen begins this novella with characteristic and infectious informality. Travel was of immeasurable importance to Andersen (1805–75), both as a private individual and as a creative writer. His first full-length work of prose was a travelogue, *Shadow Pictures*, subtitled 'From a Journey to the Harz Mountains, Saxon Switzerland etc etc in the Summer of 1831'. For all the writer's comparative youth, it shows a remarkable ability to evoke the past and the inherited culture of places alongside their ongoing present life, which he renders both in general terms and through acute observations of people encountered. Andersen even gives us glimpses into the future – he notes the formidable military installations in Prussia. Nor does he leave himself out of his 'pictures'. He hints that he has decided to go abroad for the first time because of unrequited love. In truth, he had fallen for a friend's sister, inevitably of a higher social class than himself. The situation had brought home to him just how much of an outsider he still was in the Danish upper and upper-middle class that had adopted him, paid for his education, and launched him as a writer – a feeling that stayed with him even within the family he cared for most, the Collins. How could it not be so? Back in Odense (away from the Copenhagen where he was now living and finding his literary feet) his mother was an illiterate alcoholic washerwoman, while he had lost his beloved father at the age of eleven, a shoemaker, a broken man who had served in Denmark's disastrous pro-Napoleon campaign. On his deathbed Andersen's father said of the elaborate frost patterns on his window-panes that they were signs the Ice Virgin was coming to fetch him. His son never forgot these words any more than he forgot what it felt like to love above one's station.

Andersen's prodigious gifts and his own extraordinary belief in them both impressed almost everybody he came into contact with, from his earliest childhood onwards, and also aroused feelings of irritation, resentment and jealousy. Leaving his native city for Copenhagen at the age of fourteen, with virtually no money, he was almost unbelievably forward for one so young and so undereducated in procuring introductions to leading figures in the world of the arts. The theatre was his great passion, and the Danish Royal Theatre's Director, Jonas Collin, also a counsellor at court, was sufficiently convinced of Andersen's talents to have him educated by means of a royal fund set aside to assist those showing promise. Jonas Collin also admitted him into his own family. It was Jonas's second son Edvard who brought out in Andersen feelings of warm friendship indistinguishable from love. At times this was a source of great embarrassment to Edvard. And while Andersen may have felt that – through the Collins particularly – he had arrived in Copenhagen society, that society itself, including indeed the young Collins, didn't by any means always concur. This was a situation with often very painful consequences which informed his whole life and was a major reason for travel being so strong a psychological need.

Andersen's 1831 trip set a pattern for many later journeys. Momentously, and again compelled abroad by unhappiness at home, centring indeed on Edvard Collin, Andersen travelled in 1833–34 to Paris, to French-speaking Switzerland and so down to Italy, which overwhelmed him. In Rome he associated with members of the Scandinavian Club, many of them young practitioners of the arts. One of these, Thomas Fearnley (1802–42), was a Norwegian painter of English extraction. An amorist himself, he tried without success to make Andersen more adventurous in his approach to the opposite sex. He also passed on to him his own enthusiasm for alpine scenery. Fearnley's great canvases – 'The Wetterhorn', 'Near Meiringen' (both 1835) and 'The Grindelwald Glacier' (1838) – pay homage to major natural features that were to play essential roles in Andersen's own alpine novella; indeed the Wetterhorn and Grindelwald are named in its first paragraph. Andersen's own descriptions have something of that awe, that reverence for both the blind power and the spiritually nourishing beauty of these mountains that Fearnley gave them in his paintings.

Andersen returned to Denmark in spring 1835 with two completed books that would change not only his own life but European literature itself. The first was a novel, *The Improvisatore*, which purports to be the autobiography of a young Italian born and raised in a poor quarter of Rome, and now well-known for his powers of improvisation – then a fashionable art. *The Improvisatore* shows its real author's extraordinary empathy with those outside his own culture. In *The Ice Virgin* Rudy is a chamois-hunter, a cooper, a mountain guide. And through him we learn of other representative Swiss pursuits – goat-herding, the making and selling of toy chalets, running a timber-mill, opening hotels to cater for tourists. We feel Andersen must have known such practices and customs from his own experiences. But in truth his accounts of them are the fruits of the imaginative identification he constantly made with places and a whole diversity of persons throughout his travels.

The second book that followed Andersen's return from his great European journey was his first book of *Fairy-Tales Told for Children* (*Eventyr, Fortalte for Børn*) published only a matter of weeks after *The Improvisatore*, in May 1835. Two of these fairy-tales, 'The Tinder-Box' and 'The Princess on the Pea', are still universal favourites. Andersen's faithful and kind-hearted older mentor, the distinguished physicist and writer H. C. Ørsted, told him that whereas *The Improvisatore* would make him famous (it certainly did), the fairy-tales would make him immortal, so fresh, so original, so direct were they, yet with such skilled artistry behind them. And so it has turned out, and it is as a writer of fairy-tales that Andersen is primarily thought of outside Denmark today, especially fairy-tales for children. But in fact by the time he had reached his critical and commercial breakthrough collection of 1843, *New Fairy-tales* (*Nye Eventyr*), he had dropped the qualifier 'for children' – ironically since this particular book contains one of the best-loved children's tales of all time, 'The Ugly Duckling' – and for subsequent volumes he often preferred the term *Historier* or 'Stories' rather than *Eventyr*. The reading world outside Denmark has tended to concentrate so exclusively on the children's tales that it passes by many works of great intensity and imaginative ambition in which Andersen combined the immediacy of those early tales with a complexity of construction as intricate as any in nineteenth-century fiction. Such works unite a novelist's interest in society and culture, and in the individual's relation to them, with the fairy-tale teller's way of appealing to feelings and notions well below the surface of conscious life. Such a work is *The Ice Virgin* (*Iisjomfruen*). Here we should also see Andersen's admiration for contemporaneous German writers excelling in the novella form, particularly two with whom he became friendly as far back as his tour of 1831, Ludwig Tieck (1773–1853) and Adelbert von Chamisso (1781–1838). It is my own opinion, strengthened by attentive readings of *The Ice Virgin* over many years, that Andersen never more completely realised the many aspects of his phenomenal genius than he did in this story, and that the novella form, in distinction to the full-length novel or the single-narrative tale, peculiarly assisted this richness combined with succinctness: the homely details of life in rural and small-town Switzerland, the perception of social changes and their effects on persons who cannot withstand them, the apprehension of the natural world amounting to rapport with it, from swallows and cats and an old dog to the terrifyingly inimical realms of snow, ice, flood and storm. We face up to the complex issues the tale raises, about self and civilisation, by means of its complex verbal richness, its controlled abundance of psychically penetrative imagery, its narrative that never once loses metaphoric force and its haunting ambivalence of emotional loyalties.

By the time he came to write *The Ice Virgin*, Andersen was
a writer of international stature whose travels reflected this,
being treated as a celebrity wherever he went and meeting
the leading European intellectuals and artists of the day,
Mendelssohn, Balzac, Hugo, Heine, Dickens. But in a vital
sense the Andersen who went back to Switzerland in 1861, a
country with enormous appeal for him, retained many of the
salient qualities of the young traveller he had once been. He
had proved unable – and surely at any deep level unwilling –
to unite his life with that of another person, of either sex. He
was the most stalwart of friends, however, just as he was the
most loyal of Danes, and Edvard Collin was still the most
important person in his life, even if Andersen had steadied
his expression of it. He showed his continuing devotion to
Edvard now through friendship with his wife, Jette, who was
very attached to him, and with his son Jonas. In 1861, in Italy
and Switzerland, Andersen took Jonas Collin jnr (1840–
1905), as he had done on earlier expeditions, as his travelling companion, a source of pleasure, since Andersen was
genuinely fond of him, and of vexation. Jonas, a burgeoning
biologist, was intelligent, good-looking, strong-willed, also
recalcitrant, truculent, sometimes downright insolent, and
certainly not above reminding Andersen of how indebted
he was to his grandfather, Jonas Collin snr. Some of these
attributes can be found in Rudy; *The Ice Virgin* surely gains
in authenticity from its accurately observant, feelingly done
depiction of a young man (in some ways Rudy is *every* young
male) emerging into life. He wants everything his own way,
from being the champion in the Interlaken shooting contest
to winning the hand of the beautiful daughter of one of the
richest burghers of his own region. And yet we cannot feel,

for all that a fine wedding lies ahead of him, that Rudy's ideas of his future are capable of being realised.

Andersen began this novella – to which he first gave the working title 'The Alpine Hunter' – on 18 June 1861 in a hotel in Montreux on Lake Geneva, where he and Jonas stayed until 22 June. They had journeyed there from Italy via the Simplon Pass and St Maurice in Canton Valais and Bex on the other side of the Rhône in Canton Vaud. It is a route with which readers of *The Ice Virgin* become intimately familiar, from the sharp upward bend 'like an elbow' that the river valley takes before reaching these two opposite towns to the mountain looming above Bex called Les Diablerets, the highest point in Canton Vaud. Andersen was thus staying in the very milieu with which his novella concludes, the Switzerland of resorts and luxurious hotels and international travellers, the country that Babette has been educated to appreciate and which her English godmother likes to visit, and in which, by contrast, Rudy, scion of the high Alps, is greatly ill-at-ease – and in which indeed he dies, on the eve of (apparent) happiness.

Rudy is on his mother's side of Germanophone Bernese Oberland stock. His wood-carver grandfather came from Meiringen and then made his home near Grindelwald. Rudy's father was a mail-coach man from the predominantly French-speaking and Roman Catholic Canton Valais, and it is in his Valais village that Rudy was born. After his father's death, Rudy's mother decides to take him, still a baby less than a year old, to her own father's house in the Oberland. It is on the highest point of the journey there, on the fault-line between Rudy's two ancestral regions, that the mother and her son fall into the icy chasm of the glacier, the former to her death and the latter kissed, though not to death, by the Ice Virgin, an experience with a permanent and mortal legacy. After his early childhood years in the Oberland Rudy will spend the greater part of his all-too-short life in Valais, but on his triumphant visit to the Oberland resort of Interlaken the locals think he speaks German exactly as spoken in the neighbourhood. He can therefore – not least because of his youth and dashing charm – seemingly straddle both sides of Swiss life, the German and the French, though he does not live long enough for this to be put to any test.

Rudy's story can be read, among other things, as a paradigm of Switzerland, and through the cultural differences that this entails, it stands for abiding contrasts and tensions in the human personality itself: quest versus peaceful stasis, adventure involving danger and threat to life (one's own, the lives of others) versus harmonious living, even libidinous release versus home-creating love. Not for nothing does Andersen make Rudy a skilled marksman, like the most famous Swiss of all, honoured in legend and opera, William Tell. Tell's feat is in fact commemorated in the weather-vane that surmounts Rudy's future father-in-law's mill-house.

We learn that Rudy dies in 1856, so must have been born c.1833. The action of the novella therefore takes place in a country the peace and growing prosperity of which was viewed by the rest of Europe – especially after the Swiss Federal Constitution of 1848 – as a template for other societies. More and more visitors, as is made clear in the novella, came from elsewhere to Switzerland for the sake of its spectacular natural beauties, in the interests of their mental and physical health, both catered for in its resorts, and also to experience its smooth-running societal achievements. But Andersen was aware – as all the characters of the novella are, and as a good proportion of his readers must have been – that Switzerland's recent history was not quite the serene one its present appearance suggested. Also that there might well be a downside to the galvanising transformations Switzerland had witnessed in only a few decades and which the admiring world might do well to ponder. Were there casualties as well as the many beneficiaries of so rapid and thoroughgoing a progress? Is it right that Rudy – who unquestionably arouses our sympathies – should feel so uncomfortable, so unwanted in a place like Montreux?

Andersen, as was his practice, worked with great thoroughness on *The Ice Virgin* so that topographically and historically it possesses an exemplary exactitude. Accordingly, examination of the facts behind the story is well worth making. Switzerland's long-famous cantonal system was dismantled by victorious Revolutionary France in 1798, to be replaced by a centralised government. But the subsequent Helvetic Republic was so unpopular that many Swiss refused to fight for it on the side of France, causing Napoleon to grant the Swiss their canton system back in 1803. But in the novella's course we meet one very great enthusiast for Napoleonic France, Rudy's uncle, not, for all his kindness to Rudy himself, a wholly admirable figure but an influential one. (He insists on Rudy being educated in Canton Valais, imbued, one imagines, with a belief in the inherent superiority of a French education over all others.) The post-Napoleonic Congress of Vienna of 1815 confirmed Switzerland's independence and neutrality. However, within its borders all was not completely well; the internal

differences, cultural, religious, linguistic, which the country
was in principle upholding could assert themselves, and
nowhere was this more in evidence than in the Rhône Valley,
where Cantons Valais and Vaud meet and where we readers
of *The Ice Virgin* spend so much of our time. St Maurice,
the bridge from which leads from Valais into Vaud and
which Rudy crosses bound for Bex and Babette, saw in 1847
troops of Valais soldiers amassed with the express intention
of launching an attack on Bex. Rudy's (and his paternal
family's) Canton Valais, together with six other strongly
Catholic and Conservative cantons, had united in 1843 to
form the Sonderbund (Separate Alliance) in protest against
the anti-Catholic measures of the central government. In
contrast Canton Vaud, the miller and Babette's canton,
was – and still is – overwhelmingly Protestant, conserv-
ing a legacy from Calvin's Geneva. The Sonderbundskrieg
(Sonderbund War) against the Swiss Federal Army broke
out in November 1847, but lasted a mere 26 days, with fewer
than a hundred killed and all the wounded cared for. Canton
Valais was perhaps the most committed to war of all the
Sonderbund, and was the last of its cantons to surrender.
All this – after all only in the main story's recent past –
has considerable bearing on Rudy's dealings with Babette
and the miller. It is why they have to reassure themselves
that, both being Francophone, their respective two cantons
make good neighbours, something hopefully propitious for
a good relationship between the two young people. And
the miller is surely Vaudois Protestant, having chosen an
English godmother for his daughter. When we meet this
cultivated, upper-class lady, we cannot believe she is other
than a respected member of the Church of England, and

therefore Rudy and Babette's wedding ceremony might well have taken place in an Anglican church in Montreux.

Rudy the alpine hunter? We know that the miller loves hearing from him about his chamois-hunting triumphs, the audacious skills his uncle developed in him after realising his natural talents for the pursuit. Rudy has, after all, exhibited an interest in the hunt even as a small child in the Oberland; he was more interested in the gun on a chalet roof-beam than in all the exquisite carvings in wood. He is thus more nephew of his pro-Napoleon huntsman uncle than he is grandson of the Germanophone old wood-carver. But, married to Babette, will such a risk-taking life be possible for him, or will his youthful feats be eventually consigned to a past as remote as that of the dungeons at Chillon, souvenirs of a bygone era which bore the young man stiff when he has to take part in sight-seeing? Questions now press on us. Which do we in honesty prefer, the liveliness, the enterprise, the animal good spirits, the instinctual courage and the ready resourcefulness of Rudy – most strikingly shown in his wonderfully described trek over the mountains to Interlaken in the Oberland from his village in the Valais (probably, a look at a map suggests, near Leuk) – or the second-hand, second-rate, sybaritic life-style of Babette's godmother's family in their quarters in Montreux? To say nothing of the dandyish self-satisfaction of the English cousin? And how do we view Rudy, if not favourably, alongside Babette's chatter and arch little attempts to win male admiration? But this of course is to be unfair on her. Andersen makes quite clear the sincerity not only of her love but of her high regard for Rudy. And these feelings for him bring out an unexpectedly mature percipience in her. No section of the novella is more remarkable in its insights into the wellsprings of human nature than chapter 14, 'Visions in the Night'. In this Babette perceives the fundamental incompatibility of the two of them, seeing Rudy as a decoy figure, an alpenstock hung with hunting clothes, while the frivolous English cousin – whom she doesn't even like – is restored to her company.

This 'vision' leads us to make a difficult acknowledgement. We are forced to admit that while there is much in Rudy to find attractive, even endearing, there is also much to cause us concern, for we can view him as instinctively antipathetic (possibly even antagonistic) to an enlightened, expanding modern culture, one admirable however limited. It never occurs to him that hunting chamois – which appeals to him even before he has tried it – causes suffering, brings about in truth re-enactments of that very tragedy which has scarred his own life: a mother's death, a bewildered off-spring's orphaning. This point is brought most fully home in the chapter entitled 'The Eagle's Nest', which was the second title that Andersen used for the story while at work on it. Of course we cannot but be impressed by the courage and ingenuity Rudy displays throughout this daring adventure. But how cruel it surely is deliberately to arrange the death of the magnificent mother-bird, and how acutely the hostility and distress of the captured eaglet are conveyed to us in the subsequent chapter, when Rudy brings it, caged and fiercely resentful, into the miller's house! For all his male health and confidence, Rudy is a servant of death in these seminal episodes. That there is anyway an important dark side to his whole being is inescapably revealed in the two encounters he has, alone in the mountains, with female envoys (as one assumes) of the Ice Virgin herself. These surely show that his sexual nature at the deepest level refuses to be satisfied with so domestic, so unalloyedly sweet a relationship as that to be experienced with Babette. We recall that in his infancy he was kissed by the Ice Virgin. And it was after that powerful figure that Andersen eventually chose to name the entire novella.

What does she mean? How should we interpret the kiss the Virgin gives Rudy? Ambiguity is of the story's very essence, we truly murder it to dissect. The Ice Virgin, in my view, is a personification rather than a personage, an embodiment of knowledge and of forces within ourselves that we are all obliged to recognise at some point in our lives, though how we deal with that recognition depends on our circumstances, our cultural conditioning, and, obviously, on other aspects of our personality. The Ice Virgin is an enemy of all attempts to domesticate or harness Nature, and we readers, like Andersen himself, who was deeply committed to progress, who celebrated railways and underwater cables, fear and loathe her annunciations of destruction to all human enterprises of this kind. But we also sense her incontestable indomitability, her stunning inviolable majesty, as when we look at the mountain peaks or hearken to the elemental forces we shall never be able wholly to subdue. Indeed, we live by courtesy of them every day of our lives. Rudy is one of those marked out to appreciate this truth, yet his appreciation of it denies him the life of contentment that most of us (including, for a while, himself) aspire to. And that is why Andersen, after describing what can only be termed Rudy's unavoidable, if surprised, surrender to death, and, more tentatively, his removal from the world in which he has hoped to achieve happiness to the indefinable realm of eternity, asks us: 'Would you call that a sorrowful story?' Readers must do as Andersen bids them and answer this for themselves, no easy matter – on the contrary, a profoundly challenging one. And surely a rewarding one also.

Paul Binding,
Bishop's Castle, Shropshire,
August 2016